LAST WISHES

Also by Brian David Floyd

The Class of '87 (with Robert Slawsby)

Cloning Elvis

Dad Was Right: 10 Life Lessons a Father Taught His Son

The Short Stack: Four Short Stories and One Random Poem

Learn more about Brian and get free stories at
BrianDavidFloyd.com

LAST WISHES

Brian David Floyd

This is a work of fiction. Names, characters, businesses, places, events, locales, and incidents are either the products of the author's imagination or used in a fictitious manner. Any resemblance to actual persons, living or dead, or actual events is purely coincidental.

Cover design by Rocío Martin Osuna.

First Edition

ISBN: 978-0-578-63520-0

For Gerri

Who told me to write the damn story.

A brother offended is harder to be won than a strong city:
and their contentions are like the bars of a castle.

Proverbs 18:19

EVERYTHING HAPPENS FOR A REASON.

That's what people like to say whenever anything bad happens in life.

But have you ever noticed they never seem to know exactly *why* everything bad has happened?

Is it because God has a cruel sense of humor? That's what Depeche Mode sang. Could it be because the universe came from chaos and remains that way? Stephen Hawking might agree with that sentiment. Or maybe it's a glitch in the Matrix our AI overlords refuse to fix? After all, Agent Smith did say we couldn't handle a world where life is always going good.

Honestly, none of those options work for me. Because unlike everyone else out there, I do in fact know the reason behind every horrible thing that's ever happened in my life.

It's my younger brother Billy.

That prick was placed here on planet Earth for one reason alone—to thoroughly ruin my life and drain it of happiness whenever possible.

Don't believe me? Think I'm being a drama queen who's over-sensationalizing normal sibling rivalry?

You'll see. I'm not.

PART I

The Call Home

1

I WAS MOMENTS AWAY FROM starting a new project when the biggest Billy Bomb I'd ever experienced went off and blew my life to pieces once again.

It was a Saturday night.

Technically, that's wrong. Saturday had turned into Sunday morning as it was close to one a.m.

My band and I had just wrapped up our rendition of "The Devil Went Down to Georgia" to close out the last set. No matter what era of country a person preferred, or if they hated country music, everyone loved that Charlie Daniels classic. In a tourist magnet like Gilly's, that kept people happy, dancing, and, most importantly, buying drinks.

"Let's give it up for Danny Mack and the Texas Renegades!" the DJ told the drunk, cheering crowd over the loudspeakers. "They'll be back here tomorrow night starting at nine. Right along with our world-famous bikini bull riding!"

I unplugged my Strat and put it away in its case. Big Paul, who'd been my bass player since I'd started this band, came over with a wicked grin on his face.

"You see that redhead about ready to bust out of her top?" he asked.

"Kinda hard to miss," I said, and that was the truth.

She stood at the railing on the far side of the dance floor, drinking a bottle of Blue Moon. I put her in the late twenties, maybe early thirties. Red, curly hair, probably from a bottle, but her skin was pale enough that it could've been natural. She wore a tight-fitting white tank top and jeans meant to show off her already eye-catching curves. Like her red hair, the assets she proudly displayed could have been real or enhanced.

I planned to get the answer to both questions before the sun rose.

I'd noticed Project Redhead not long after she'd entered the bar. Every hetero male in the place had too. But that was all planned. The way she dressed and walked, she wanted to be noticed. She'd come in at the beginning of the final set by herself, making it impossible to miss her arrival.

I'd already picked out a couple of possible contenders for tonight's project. A woman I put in her early forties celebrating her divorce sitting with her friends over by the mechanical bull. They all had on customized T-shirts like it was her bachelorette party.

The other contender was the woman with the short hair from New York I'd talked to during our last break. She'd asked me to play a Brad Paisley tune in the next set.

I politely lied and told her the request list was full for the night. I didn't typically like hair that short, but she had intense blue eyes and a great smile, so I could make an exception.

Both seemed like they'd be fun projects, but Red quickly moved to the top of the potential list.

As we played, I'd kept my eyes on Red as she stood at the rail without giving the impression I was doing so. With beautiful women if you jump too fast, you're burnt toast. On top of that, I had to make sure she wasn't with a guy who might be out at a craps table. Or worse, that she was a working girl. Hookers typically didn't troll Gilly's, but it was still Vegas. You never could be sure.

During our final set, a few brave souls wandered over to ask her to dance. All got shot down. That proved my point about being too eager but also, more importantly, that she wasn't on the job.

After three songs, I finally let my eyes meet hers full-on. Project Redhead held my stare, then looked away. I didn't. I kept looking straight at her until she looked back up at me. This time a flirtatious smile curved up at the corners of her lips. Yep, this red-headed kitten had come out to play.

"Think they're bolt-ons or originals?" Big Paul asked me as I clasped the latches on my guitar case closed. He was one of those rare happily married men. Yet he still enjoyed hearing my stories and living vicariously through my projects.

My fiddle player Rusty answered his question before I could. "I'll be sure to let you know."

"Whoa, Junior," I said to Rusty. "You think you have a chance with her?"

"It's already a done deal," Rusty said.

"Oh, really?"

"She couldn't keep her eyes off me this entire set."

"You really need to cut back the drinking while you're playing. It was me she was looking at," I told Rusty.

"If that's what you think, you probably should schedule an appointment with your eye doctor."

I turned to Big Paul. "Can you believe this guy?"

Paul smiled at my comment and remained silently neutral.

Rusty was the youngest member of the band, recently turned twenty-four. His face was covered with the kind of thick beard that Zac Brown had re-popularized. On top of his musical talents as a guitarist and fiddler, Rusty had impressed me with the decent record he'd had with the ladies since joining us. It was almost as good as mine. But Project Redhead was out of his league.

"Look," Rusty said to me. "If you think you have a shot, feel free to take a crack at her."

I smiled at Rusty. "I don't need any charity, kid. But you can thank me for stopping you from embarrassing yourself with her."

2

"HOWDY," I SAID, SIDLING UP beside Project Redhead, then taking a sip of the ice-cold water I'd picked up at the bar before making my approach.

She didn't reply. I briefly wondered if she'd heard me over the music. Odds were that she did but was testing me, pretending not to hear me to see if she could draw me into repeating my greeting. I didn't take her bait. After a moment, she turned her head slightly in my direction.

"Howdy?" she asked. "That's not too original for a country bar."

She spoke without any regional accent that stood out to me. She must've been a West Coaster too.

"Well, my band does play mostly covers," I said.

"And that means you don't have to be original?"

"Nope. I just gotta be good."

She stared at me, seeming to decide whether to show me contempt or interest, before saying, "Oh, and are you?"

"Haven't had any beer bottles chucked at me in some time."

"Sounds like a dangerous job."

"Somewhat. But it also adds to the fun of it."

"So, you like having fun?"

"It's one of my two favorite things to have."

"And what might the other be?"

Bam. I had this fishy on the line.

Still, I had to reel her in slow or risk her breaking loose.

"Oh," I said, feigning modesty. "It wouldn't be appropriate to say something like that to a lady I just met."

"Then I suppose we should get to know each other better."

"I'm Danny," I said, offering her my hand.

She took it and said, "I heard. Danny Mack."

"Meacham, actually. Mack's more of a stage name."

"Would you prefer to know my stage name or my real name?"

Wait a minute. Was she a stripper?

No, of course not.

She wouldn't have been in here, not on a weekend when she could be giving lap dances to sweaty tourists and making bank.

Red was still testing me. I could do the same, and went all in.

"I'm not sure if knowing each other's names really matters tonight."

"You're probably right," she said, staring into my eyes.

There wasn't much purpose in talking any further. Project Redhead was as ready and eager to go as I was. I hoped she was staying here at the TI, because in ten minutes or less we could be undressed and doing things everyone comes to Vegas hoping to do.

Before I could make my next move, Marge, the club's overweight, over-makeup-ed, and over-nicotined entertainment manager, stepped up on the other side of the rail.

"Sorry to bother you, Danny," Marge said in her gravelly voice that had been worn down by years of chain-smoking.

"It's all right," I lied, playing it cool. "What's up?"

"Your mom called during your last set."

I felt panic rise in my chest and my heartbeat accelerated.

My mom had called? Why would she call here? No. She wouldn't. She'd call my cell.

I relaxed. Someone was playing me. I looked over to the table where my four bandmates were collaborating on making a bucket of Lone Star vanish as rapidly as possible. Rusty toasted me with his brown bottle.

"That's clever," I said to Marge. "You tell Rusty—"

Before I could finish, Marge held up a yellow Post-it Note. It read: **Danny call your mom** and listed a phone number. It had a 951 area code. I recognized the first three digits of the number. I didn't have my mom's cell memorized, since it was in my phone, but I knew that was her number.

Why hadn't she just called me?

Damn. Maybe she had.

I always turned my phone completely off when I was

playing.

I pulled my Galaxy from the back left pocket of my jeans and powered it up. As it came to life, it instantly beeped that I had a text message. It was from Mom and read:

Call As Soon As You Can. Urgent.

Mom wasn't the type to throw around words like "urgent" and "important" simply to get a quick call back.

What had happened? Had she had another heart attack?

I needed to call her back, but the music was too loud in here. I needed to get outside. But what about Project Redhead? She stood there looking at me, the flow of our flirtatious conversation interrupted by an untimely urgent message from my mother.

"Would you excuse me real quick?" I asked her. She looked me straight in the eyes for a long while, obviously trying to determine if I was worth the wait.

"Well, it is your mother," she said, then took a drink of her beer and turned away from me.

Not good. Not good at all.

But I couldn't backtrack now. Project Redhead would take that as a sign of weakness. I couldn't show that or I wouldn't get a chance to get her name or anything else from her.

Dammit.

What the hell could be so urgent, Mom?

3

"MOM, WHAT'S GOING ON?" I asked as soon as she answered. "You okay?"

"I'm fine. Nothing's wrong with me," she said.

Whew. I'd nearly given myself a heart attack worrying she'd had a second. A big one had almost taken my mom out about ten years ago. Open-heart surgery and a long, slow recovery followed. While she'd made pretty significant lifestyle changes since, that didn't really cancel out her chances of having another one.

I breathed a little easier knowing that Mom was fine. Her timing sucked, but at least she was okay. I should've known she was. If something terrible had happened to Mom, it would have been my sister Tina who got ahold of me. What had made Mom's urgent request for a call now became apparent.

"What happened to Dad?" I asked.

Although they'd been divorced for probably ten years now, something bizarre continued to connect my parents. Guess that was what happened when you were married for thirty years, even if they never loved each other for any of them. Still, if tragedy ever befell Dad, I knew it would be Mom who would break the news to me.

"Your father's fine," she said. "Well, as fine as he can be."

"Then what's going on?"

Mom didn't answer immediately, but when her words came out, I knew why she'd hesitated.

"It's Billy. He's been in an awful accident."

Unbelievable. That was her urgent news? You'd think that after all this time she'd know I couldn't care less about what happened to the Prick.

"He's had accidents before," I said. More than any person I knew.

"Not like this."

Mom's voice broke as she said it. I heard her sobbing. I remained silent. Billy wasn't worth anyone's tears. Not hers. Definitely not mine. No one's.

I turned away from the TI and took in the Vegas Strip. The traffic wasn't too heavy on the boulevard. It seldom was up here, especially at that hour. Once you got down to Caesars, the congestion typically started.

After another few seconds of crying, Mom composed herself and said, "Danny, you need to come home."

The hell I did.

"Mom, I can't just up and leave. I've got a gig tomorrow night."

"But Danny, Billy's in really bad shape."

"My being there isn't going to change that."

"You don't understand. We really need you here."

"And I really don't know how I'd pull it off. Even if I wanted to come down, I've got a gig tomorrow night. I can't just be a no-show."

Silence once more. I should have said goodbye, ended the call, and gone back inside to Project Redhead. But Mom started sobbing again. I couldn't hang up. She pulled it together faster this time and said the words I'd hoped she wouldn't.

"Danny, I really need you here. Please… do it for me."

4

I WENT BACK INSIDE GILLY'S with my mind running in a million directions. None of them on the one thing that mattered—getting Project Redhead undressed and horizontal without further delay. With the pressure Mom had just applied to me, I was going to need some vigorous sexual fulfillment now more than before.

But first I had to get things covered for Sunday night's gig.

I found Big Paul, Butch, and Jackson at the high-top table near the mechanical bullring where they'd started in on a new bucket of beer.

Big Paul noticed me first. He'd been playing with me the longest and was the closest thing to a best friend I had made since moving to Vegas. He must've read my internal anguish from my face and body language.

"Everything all right?" he asked.

"Family shit," I said, having zero desire to get into the details.

Big Paul nodded his understanding. Butch my bass player and Jackson my drummer turned their attention to me, not looking for more info. They most likely were curious as to why I was standing at their table instead of leaving with Project Redhead.

The same question went through my mind. I decided to cut to the chase.

"If I had to go to California for a couple days, would that be all right?"

"What about our gig tonight?" Butch asked.

"I was thinking that Rusty could take the lead for the night... if you all were good with that."

Jackson shrugged. "I ain't got a problem with it."

"Me neither," Butch said.

"Family always comes first," Big Paul said. "Take whatever time you need."

"It's only for a day. I'll be back by Monday," I said. "Thanks, guys. I'll clear it with Marge." I looked at the empty chair. "Rusty still around, or did he find himself a skank for the night?"

Butch lifted his beer, raised it high, and downed its contents. Big Paul looked down at the table, picking at a hangnail on his thumb. Only Jackson met my eyes.

"Looks like he's about to leave," Jackson said. "But I'm not so sure how much of a skank she is."

I spun to my right, looking back to the railing where I'd left Project Redhead. She wasn't there.

No! She hadn't left. She must be in the bathroom.

I quickly scanned the bar. I spotted Rusty first, then I saw the redhead. She was holding his hand as they sauntered past the bouncer at the main door and out into the casino.

"That little son of a bitch," I unintentionally said out loud.

"Looks like he really is ready to fill in for you," Jackson said.

Butch, Big Paul, and Jackson laughed hard at my expense. My temperature flared to boiling. I had a crazy thought of running after them, tackling Rusty from behind, beating him senseless, and taking her back. Project Redhead had been mine!

No. She'd *almost* been mine. I'd failed to close thanks to that message from Mom.

No. It wasn't Mom's fault either, though she'd been an unwitting accomplice.

It was the damn Billy's fault. Just like always.

5

I HAD NO IDEA WHAT to do with myself. And doing something with *myself* was not an option. For the first time in a long time, I'd left a gig without a project.

That's a bit of an exaggeration, but not much. It was more like the first weekend night that I didn't have a project. Almost every weekend my band played at Gilly's, Toby Keith's, or sometimes Sam's Town. While the quality of the projects would vary based on the location, there were always projects to be had when we played. It was Vegas, after all. The term "ready and willing" felt like an understatement when describing the women who came to town. Being a musician just made it like throwing dynamite into a barrel of fish.

After Rusty hijacked Project Redhead, I looked around for Short Hair but didn't see her. I did find the divorce party, but the divorcee at that point was no longer an option. Two of her friends held her up between them as they headed to the door, as this newly single woman had now lost her ability to walk.

I briefly considered asking one of the waitresses I

frequently flirted with if she wanted to "Netflix and chill," even though I didn't currently subscribe to Netflix. I quickly decided against it. Hookups always led to complications when you got with a woman who worked under the same roof as you. Even if it happened just for some good-hearted recreational sex. I'd learned that one the hard way a couple times.

Without Netflix and only having basic cable, there wasn't anything on the TV that interested me. I tried to watch an episode of that new show *Live PD*. It's always fun to watch an idiot who thinks it's a smart idea to run from the police. That is until a hungry K-9 or a supercharged Taser takes them down. But I wasn't in the mood.

I went to bed but couldn't sleep. After the longest time of tossing, turning, and refusing to masturbate, I grabbed my phone off the nearby table. It was 4:06 and I was wide-awake. "Screw it," I said. I got out of bed, took a quick shower, and got dressed.

I threw a pair of underwear, socks, a shirt, and a fresh pair of Wranglers into my duffel bag. From the bathroom, I added my toothbrush, my half-used tube of Colgate, and dental floss. I naturally packed deodorant but opted to not take any condoms. I wouldn't be down long enough to find any projects. Not that I'd want to hook up with anyone back home anyway.

I went back into my bedroom and considered grabbing my Martin acoustic guitar for the trip. It would help me kill time and avoid talking more than I had to with my family. I decided against taking it. I wouldn't be down south that long.

Duffel over my shoulder, I went to the refrigerator and grabbed the last two cans of Diet Dr. Pepper and headed out the door. I threw my bag in the back of my Outlander.

Ugh. I couldn't believe I was doing this. I pulled up my 90's Country playlist on Spotify, headed to I-15, and drove south.

It might only be twenty-four hours and change back home, but I dreaded the thought, especially with Billy being the reason I had to come down. Maybe I'd get lucky and even be able to pull off a turnaround trip, get back into town before eight tonight, play with the band, and pick up a project. After all, tonight was bikini bull riding. More than a few potential projects would be coming in for that.

Yeah, it was all wishful thinking, but I had to have something to think about to keep my mind off the fact that I'd be coming face to face with my prick brother for the first time in twelve years.

I'd been twenty-five years old when I left Norco. I hadn't had any contact with the Prick or anyone outside of my family since I'd moved away. Despite going down there at various times of the year for Christmas and Mom's birthday, I'd never looked back.

I'd made Mom, Dad, and Tina swear not to give Billy my phone number. He couldn't reach out to me on Facebook because I was one of the few Americans not using it or any of the other social media fads. I'd cut the

Prick out of my life entirely and was happy. I should have known there was no way he'd ever let that last.

I'd feared it would happen here in Vegas. I just wasn't far enough away from him. I figured one night the Prick would walk into one of the bars where my band was playing. There'd be nothing I could do about it. Given that Vegas was the perfect place for someone to get liquored up and get a pass for acting like a complete jackass, I'd expected he'd pop up one of these nights.

Somehow, that dreaded reunion never happened.

Instead, I found myself going to see the Prick on my own volition. If Mom hadn't called and tearfully asked me to come, it wouldn't be happening. No way. No how. No sir.

I couldn't help but wonder what had happened to him.

Had Billy gone through the windshield, eviscerated his face, and become unrecognizable? Was he crushed inside a car, breaking every bone in his body and put into a full-body cast? Or maybe when he crashed a sharp piece of metal penetrated his car and came up through his seat and castrated him in an excruciatingly painful manner?

Each of those fantasies was enjoyable to entertain. Whatever happened to Billy, the one thing I knew with absolute certainty was that the Prick deserved it.

As I came out of the foothills and left the vast desert I'd crossed in mostly darkness, the early signs of a beautiful day appeared. The air wasn't tinged as brown as it would be in the warmer months of the year. It even looked mostly blue. Growing up here in the so-called Inland Empire, you pretty much accepted smog for air. It was only after my first tour that I realized how filthy the sky was back home.

I turned off Spotify and switched over to the radio to listen to K-FROG. That country station had been going strong since I was a kid, and it remained my favorite. Back in the day, a couple of the DJs who went by the on-air names of Heather Froglear and Jimmy Hoppa had helped a my band at the time, The Regulators, get a gig at the Brandin' Iron. That led to some fantastic opportunities for us, but that wasn't something I wanted to think about.

A few minutes later, I switched freeways and went north on the 10. Mom had told me that Billy was at Loma Linda. While the hospital's name might sound quaint and peaceful, it conjured up much darker emotions for those of us raised in the IE. Loma Linda was where they took patients, sometimes by airlift, when their injuries were so severe that none of the other hospitals could provide the treatment needed.

Family stories had it that this was where they took Billy when he'd been born six weeks premature. Now here he was thirty-four years later. Maybe there was something to the whole circle of life thing, Simba.

I parked in the visitor lot and looked to the hospital complex, wondering which of the numerous buildings I'd find the Prick in. I'd go through the closest door and hope that was it. If not, I'd ask someone who worked there where I could find the intensive care unit.

It turned out I didn't have to. I got out of my Outlander as a canary-yellow Corvette zoomed into the parking space to the right of my car. A familiar man with long, greying hair tied back in a ponytail got out of the car and smiled at me.

"Danny Boy!" he said.

I'd always hated him calling me that.

"Hey, Dad," I said.

6

DAD CAME OVER AND SHOOK my hand. We didn't have a huggy relationship.

"How was the drive down?" he asked.

"I didn't crash."

"Yeah, that's good," Dad said, not catching my not-quite-tasteful reply. "I'm surprised to see you so early."

"Yeah, I never really went to bed."

Dad gave me a sly smile and a wink. "That's my boy."

I couldn't dissuade Dad from the notion that I hadn't gotten any sleep because I'd been with someone last night. But discussing my nocturnal social habits with him wasn't something I wanted to do either. I decided to take things the serious route.

"Mom didn't really get into any details when she called. What exactly happened to Billy?"

Dad looked down at the pavement for a few seconds, then back up at me. He seemed to be thinking about how to answer what I thought was a straightforward question.

"Your sister's probably the best person to explain it. Let's go inside."

Tina was already here too? My neck and shoulders tightened. Billy must've really done a number on himself this time.

"Okay," I said, and allowed Dad to lead me into the hospital.

I'd hoped that we'd be able to walk in silence, but Dad was not someone who could handle any kind of quiet, so he went into one of his customary topics. Music.

"Did you happen to catch the Stones the last time they were on tour?"

"Can't say that I did."

"Those old limeys sure the hell can still rock. But how Keith Richards is still alive is beyond me. You know what I'm saying?"

"Good genes."

"Yeah. Him and Mick both."

Dad continued his praise of the Rolling Stones and led me into the main hospital building of Loma Linda. He seemed to know the hallways quite well. As he ushered me into a pink-wallpapered waiting room, he said in a too-excited voice, "Baby girl. Look who's here!"

My sister Tina looked up from the maroon-cushioned chair where she sat with a laptop on her knees as she typed away. She glanced up at me for a couple seconds, Mr. Spock-like. No emotion on her face. Her eyes fell back to her laptop.

Tina was a little more than a year older than me. She'd taken good care of herself and was aging well, but she was too uptight. Even though it was Sunday, she was dressed in a classy but casual blouse, with overpriced designer blue jeans, her sandy blonde hair tied up in a ponytail. Dad and I must've looked like bums standing beside her. She always was meticulous about her appearance, just like everything in her life.

Tina finished what she was typing, set her computer on the chair beside her, and rose to give me her customary greeting.

"Hey there, little brother."

"Hey, big sister."

Tina put her arms around me and we shared a short hug, the kind that always seemed to be required more than wanted. As she and I stepped back from each other, I asked, "Mom here?"

"She's over in ICU," Tina said.

I should've guessed that one. No matter how big of a screw-up Billy could be, and he was a giant one, he was still her baby boy. Mom had stood by him through all of his crap. Regardless of how many people he hurt or how much he abused his relationship with Mom, she'd always love him and be at his side. I guessed it'd be the same for her with Tina or me. But Billy had always been the one who needed that extra maternal attention and support, and the Prick had always received it.

"What exactly happened?" I asked Tina.

"Well, what do you know?" she said. I sensed my question had caused a bit of discomfort in her.

"All Mom said was he was in a bad accident. We didn't get into any details."

"You know where Center dead-ends into Fifth Street?" she asked.

"Yeah." It was only about two blocks away from Mom's house.

"It looks like Billy took the corner too fast and went headfirst into a telephone pole."

"A telephone pole? Can't say that's shocking."

Dad shrugged in agreement with my sarcastic assessment.

Tina might have agreed too, but she hid it well by jumping on me for it.

"We all know Billy's had his problems," she said, "but he happens to be fighting for his life right now, so can you at least pretend to show him some compassion?"

"Hey, I'm here, aren't I?"

"For once."

No. I wasn't playing Tina's game. "Just point me toward the ICU, all right?"

Seeing her ploy wasn't working, Tina changed tactics. She let the look fall from her eyes and replaced it with one of compassion. If my sister hadn't chosen a career as a lawyer, she would've made one hell of an actress.

"I'm sorry," she said. "The last week here's been rather stressful."

"Wait. What do you mean *the last week*?" I asked.

Now it was Tina's turn to look away and not answer

my questions. Dad decided to speak up and said, "Billy crashed... last Friday night."

That was, what...eight days ago?

"And Mom didn't call me till yesterday?" I asked, my voice rising as I did.

Tina answered, "She wanted to call you sooner, but given the history between you and Billy, I convinced her to wait and see what happened before she did."

Yeah, the Prick and I had *history*, all right. My entire family knew it. And now Mom had called me a week after Billy's latest accident. He'd really screwed himself up this time, hadn't he?

"Okay," I said as calmly as I could. "Exactly how bad off is he?"

Tina's eyes once again found the carpet. She said nothing. I turned to Dad. He looked over at the wall.

"Tina," I said again, "how bad is Billy?"

She looked up, but not at me. Her eyes went to Dad. "Dad, why don't you see if you can find Dr. Pettis and I'll take Danny over to ICU?"

"Sure thing, baby girl," Dad said, and was out of the room as quickly as he could go.

Something was severely wrong here. I could feel it in my stomach.

Had the dumbass gone through the windshield of his car after all?

7

I saw Mom before she saw me. My eyes stayed on her; they didn't go to Billy lying unconscious in the bed in the ICU. While I'd seen her only a few months ago after Christmas, Mom looked different now, and not in a good way. She had dark circles under her eyes and seemed to be about ten pounds lighter, which she didn't need to be. The roots of her chestnut-dyed hair were revealing her natural grey, which I'd never seen her allow before.

Tina had us buzzed into the ICU and led me past several beds of maimed or dying patients that I didn't want to look at. At the end of them all, I followed her around a curtain. There Mom sat in a chair next to Billy's bed, her oxygen machine slung over her shoulder, the clear plastic tubes running out of it and up into her nostrils.

Mom had to be put on the oxygen after five decades of committed smoking. The device she wore now allowed her greater movement and freedom, unlike the canister of oxygen she used to have to cart around at her side.

Mom must have sensed me standing there. Her head slowly turned my way. When her eyes met mine, she smiled, but it did nothing to lift the weariness she carried.

"Danny," she said, and rose from the chair with some effort.

I crossed the distance to her so she wouldn't have to expend any more energy than necessary.

"Hey, Mom," I said, and opened up my arms to hug her.

She embraced me tightly. "Thank you for coming."

"Yeah," I said, avoiding the temptation to say something sarcastic.

When Mom eventually released me, I turned toward the bed.

My imaginings about the severe physical consequences of the Prick's car accident were not realized.

He didn't look all that different than I remembered. He was older and appeared skinnier than I recalled. He had the beginnings of a beard growing on his face, probably a week's worth from lying here. Besides the physical changes, the most significant difference about him was the tubes that ran into him and out to the machines behind his bed.

One was inserted into a hole they'd cut into his neck. It ran to a machine that seemed to be keeping him breathing. A second tube went into his side. A third ran up into his crotch. Other than that, he looked like he was sleeping and nothing more.

"He doesn't look too bad," I said, but knew if they had a machine breathing for him, it was pretty damn bad despite other appearances.

Tina moved next to me. "The swelling and bruising's gone down considerably. It was a lot worse."

"So, what's exactly wrong with him?" I asked Tina.

Tina looked away and said, "It's best if the doctor explains it to you."

This really wasn't like my sister the know-it-all. I turned to Mom. She wouldn't let her eyes meet mine either.

"All right," I said. "What is everyone not telling me?"

Neither Mom nor Tina replied to my question. I turned back to the Prick to study him more closely.

There weren't any bruises, cuts, or stitches on his face. His arms were bare and neither of them was in a cast. I noticed he'd added numerous tattoos to them since our last encounter.

On his right bicep, a large cross had been inked into his skin. Ain't it funny how all the scum of the earth always wear a cross or get one tattooed on their bodies? It's like the cross deflects people from seeing all of the horrible deeds they'd inflicted on to the world.

It didn't work on me that way.

Especially when I saw on his left arm a permanent reminder of the biggest middle finger he'd ever thrown my way. In various shades of ink, etched into his skin, was a near-perfect artist's rendering of the Slut.

She looked just as I remembered her. It must've been done a decade or so ago, as it captured her perfectly back then. Beautiful. Alluring. The real slut she was.

What the hell am I even doing here?

I needed to get out of there immediately.

8

"HERE HE IS, MY BOY Danny, just come in from Vegas," Dad announced from behind me. This effectively prevented me from fleeing to my car and back to Vegas faster than I could say "Billy is a prick" fifty times.

I turned as Dad approached with a woman in her mid-forties wearing the usual white coat. She offered me a calming smile and her right hand.

"Hello, Mr. Meacham. I'm Dr. Pettis."

"Danny's fine," I said, and shook her hand firmly but lightly, as you do with a woman.

"I'm sure your family appreciates you making the trip."

"They probably do, but they still won't tell me what exactly's going on here, so hopefully you will."

The doctor wasn't ready for my bluntness. She looked at Mom, Dad, and Tina. As they had been doing with me, none of them would look her in the eye either. Dr. Pettis took a breath then looked at me as she put on her most professional demeanor.

"Why don't you tell me what you do know and I'll see if I can fill in the blank spaces?"

I pointed at the Prick lying unconscious in the bed. "All I know is he took a header into a telephone pole and has been out of it for a week now."

"Yes, your brother was involved in a very bad accident and, as a result, suffered severe head trauma. The damage is internal to the brain. He's been unconscious since he arrived. As you can see, he remains comatose with considerable brain damage."

Whoa. The Prick *had* done a real number on himself.

"Then… he's brain dead?" I asked.

"No," Tina said before the doctor could. "Billy can still breathe on his own without that ventilator."

"That is correct," Dr. Pettis cautiously said to Tina, before returning her attention to me. "However, there's more to the picture."

Tina crossed her arms and clenched her jaw. I knew that look. She was ready to pounce as soon as another word she didn't agree with came out of the doctor's mouth.

"You see, Mr. Meacham… I mean Danny," Dr. Pettis said, "your brother had a large amount of opiates in his system when he was brought in. We weren't sure if he was unresponsive due to that or the trauma caused by the impact of the collision. But now that the drugs are out of his system, he hasn't shown any signs of improvement. Therefore, we're classifying him as being in a persistent vegetative state."

And there it was.

"So, he's a vegetable?"

Tina injected herself into the conversation again. "No. He could still wake up."

"That is a possibility," the doctor said, "*but*, as I've stated, it's a remote one, in my professional opinion."

"Are you saying he's just going to stay like this forever?" I asked.

Dr. Pettis hesitated before answering my question. "As long as your brother's being provided nutrition and doesn't develop an infection or contract pneumonia, he could realistically remain in this state for several years. But our hospital doesn't provide the type of long-term care he requires."

"Billy's not going into a home," Mom said.

"Mom—" Tina said.

"You're not putting him in a home," Mom said, louder this time.

"And here we go again," Dad said.

"I'm not interested in your opinion," Mom told him.

I turned to see the three of them setting up for a Mexican standoff that reminded me of the end of *Reservoir Dogs*. Fortunately, in that movie, Tarantino's characters all blew each other away. In my family, they'd open fire with their mouths and live to spout off at each other on another day. There's really no place like home.

The best plan of action to stay out of it was to keep my focus on the doctor. She had the same idea and continued talking to me.

"As I've discussed with your family, if you choose to keep Billy on life support and are opposed to moving him to a nursing facility, he could be cared for at home with the assistance of a visiting nurse. Now, while that is an option… I do believe you need to take into account the directive your brother made about how he wants a situation such as this handled."

I had no idea what the doctor meant by that, but it completely silenced the rest of my family. Something in my gut told me not to ask a clarifying question.

I foolishly did so anyway.

"And what exactly is this medical directive he made about a situation such as this?"

My question caught the doctor by surprise. "No one's told you?"

"I can't say that they have."

I turned to Mom. She'd brought me into this mess. She could tell me what it was.

But Mom wasn't looking at me. She was digging into her purse. She pulled a thick sheaf of several pages from it and looked up at me.

"It's why you needed to come home," Mom said. She held folded papers up and toward me. "You need to read this."

9

"AND WHAT EXACTLY IS *THIS*?" I asked Mom, refusing to take the document she held out to me.

Dr. Pettis spoke before Mom could answer. I could sense her discomfort. "It appears you have a lot to discuss. I'm going to make my rounds. If you have any questions, have a nurse find me."

Without waiting for a reply, Dr. Pettis turned and took a few quick steps out of our presence. This left me standing there facing Mom, Dad, and Tina. Each of them had a different level of pain on their faces.

"Okay," I said. "What's the hell's going on here?"

Mom said, "Danny, please read this."

"Not until you tell me what the hell it is."

"It's Billy's living trust," Mom said. "You need to read it."

I pointed to Tina. "She's the lawyer, not me."

"I have read it," Tina said, "and you need to as well."

"I don't need to do anything."

"Please, Danny," Mom said, "just read it."

"That's not happening."

"You really need to," Tina said, drawing closer to Mom.

"And why's that?"

"Because Billy made you the administrator of his trust and the agent for all of his medical decisions," Tina said.

"I don't have the slightest clue what any of that means," I said, and I didn't. But I also knew that didn't sound like anything I wanted to be a part of.

Dad cut to the chase for me. "It means Billy put you in charge."

"In charge of what?"

"Everything," Mom said.

"What do you mean by everything?"

"She means *everything*," Tina said.

She took the document from Mom and flipped through it rapidly, looking for a particular page. She found it and pushed it under my nose, pointing to a section in the middle.

"Allow me to explain this so you can understand it," Tina said.

"Oh pretty please, would you?"

Tina ignored my sarcasm. "In layman's terms, Billy's given you full power of attorney. You're in charge of everything in his life now. His money. His estate. His medical decisions. He's put you in charge of all of it."

No!

This wasn't happening. It made no sense.

I hated Billy. He hated me too. Which meant the only

reason it would was because one of these three had suggested it to him. And I knew exactly which one.

"And why exactly would he do that?" I asked Tina, the anger starting to bubble out of my mouth.

"Don't look at me like that. I'm not the one who wrote this up."

"We've been over this," Mom said to Tina. "You're a prosecutor. You don't do wills."

"I still could've looked it over," Tina said.

"Billy felt more comfortable going to someone not in the family," Mom said.

"But if he'd just let her look at it," Dad said, "she never would've let him stick Danny with this."

"Just because the boys have had some issues—" Mom said.

"Some issues?" I interrupted. "It's a lot bigger than that, and you know it."

"Well, now's the time to put them aside," Mom said.

"Uh-uh. I'm not going to be the one he forces into pulling the plug."

"You don't have to," Tina said. "Billy only needs more time to heal and recover."

"Well, that's not my problem now, is it?" I said.

I turned around, pushed past Dad and out of Billy's little curtained area, heading for the door that would let me out of intensive care.

"Where you going?" Dad asked.

"Back to Vegas."

10

TINA CAUGHT UP TO ME in the main hallway, hurried a few steps in front of me, then blocked me from reaching the main doors to exit the hospital to freedom.

"I see you still run away whenever you can't handle a situation," she said.

"No, this is me handling the situation," I said.

I moved to pass her, but she grabbed my arm and pulled me to a stop. "This doesn't have to be as difficult as you're making it."

"He's the one who made it difficult. Just like he always has," I said, facing her.

"Would you please put your tantrum on hold for a minute? I don't have the first clue why he chose you—"

"'Cause the Prick always enjoys sticking it to me. That's why."

"Don't call him that. He's our brother."

"He stopped being *my* brother a long time ago, and you know it. And he knows it. There's no way I'm going to have him make me responsible for turning those machines off."

"I already told you, this isn't about turning off his life support. It's about getting Billy the care that he needs so he can recover."

"From what I heard his doctor say, that doesn't sound too likely to happen."

"People wake up from comas all the time, long after their doctors have given up on them. I know Billy will too. We just need to get him out of here and taken care of."

"Nice try, but there's no *we* here, Tina, because there's also no *me*. But I'll tell you what: as his agent or whatever the hell it's called, I give you total permission to move him into your house and take care of him."

"I can't do that."

"But he's *your* brother."

"I'm up for a big promotion right now. If I were to take leave, I could be passed over."

"And it would be so tragic if Billy screwed up *your* life for a change."

"I put off taking the bar for six months when Mom had her heart attack. What were you here for? A week?"

"Don't you dare try and guilt trip me into taking care of him."

"I'm not. But I do need you to work with me on getting care for Billy, because they can't keep him here any longer."

"The doctor said he belongs in a nursing home."

"Did it sound like Mom's going to let that happen?"

"Grandma K died from a stroke, not because Mom and

Aunt Geena put her into a home."

"Care to explain that to Mom?"

"Then Mom can take care of him. She's been doing it his entire life anyway."

"Did you see how difficult it was for her to get out of her chair? Mom can't even make it from her car to the front door without stopping to catch her breath."

"Well, without you risking your precious promotion, I guess we're all out of options."

I started for the doors again, but Tina's next words halted my escape.

"Dad's an option."

I whirled toward her. "You can't be serious."

"I wouldn't say it if I wasn't."

"He can barely take care of himself. You think he has the ability to take care of an invalid?"

"Billy's not an invalid."

"You've been a lawyer too long, because whether you want to hear this or not, right now, your baby brother is pretty much the poster child for invalidism."

Tina took slow steps toward me. "Look, Danny... I know Dad isn't the optimal choice, but he's not currently working—"

"There's another shocker."

"I've already talked with him about it. He wants to take care of Billy." Tina was now standing only a few inches from me.

"That would honestly be worse than putting Billy in a

home."

"Then what do you suggest we do?"

"I already told you. There is no *we* here."

"You're right, Danny. It's you. Because like it or not, Billy put you in charge."

Tina put her hand on my shoulder, attempting to calm me down as she continued.

"Look," she said, "as Billy's agent, you can hire a nurse to come in and take care of him. All Dad would need to do is keep an eye on him at night. There's an excellent service in Riverside. They can have a visiting nurse assigned to Billy as early as tomorrow."

The fullness of details Tina had about this made me instantly suspicious. "And how exactly do you know all that?"

"I've been doing some research into it, hoping you'd let Dad do it."

"Well, I'm not."

"And why not?"

"'Cause the Prick would probably be dead within three days even with Dad only watching him at nights."

"And Mom will probably have another heart attack or wind up in rehab again if you put Billy into a home."

"Then I like I said, we're all out of options."

"Not entirely."

Tina stared at me. She had something up her sleeve, but I didn't know what.

"Okay," I said. "Tell me what it is you're scheming."

"It's not a scheme. Just hear me out…"

"What is it?"

"You."

"Me. What do you mean me?"

"You, Danny. You're still an option."

"The hell I am."

"Just consider it."

"No need to. The answer is no."

I started for the doors again. This time I wouldn't be stopping.

"Our baby brother's life is hanging in the balance here. How can you be so selfish?" she yelled after me.

"Call it a Meacham family trait," I yelled back without turning around.

The doors electronically slid open for me. I stepped outside and headed for my car.

11

DAMN THAT TINA.

This was all her scheme from the beginning.

It had to be.

I'd made it to my Outlander, got the engine started, but didn't get out of the parking lot. I didn't even put it in reverse. My mind kept coming back to Mom. I couldn't get the picture of Mom in her quickly advancing frailty out of my mind. I imagined Marge coming up to me after a set with a message from Tina. I'd call her back and she'd tell me Billy had died... or Mom... or maybe both.

Wouldn't that be something a double funeral? All eyes would be on me, and the words wouldn't be spoken, they'd be thought. *Danny, this is all your fault.*

Damn that Tina. She'd planted that seed in my head and I couldn't get rid of it. I bet she'd even told Mom to call me last night, knowing that's what it would take to bring me home. I needed to put the car in reverse and get the hell out of there.

Instead, I pulled my phone out of my pocket and called Big Paul's. His cell went to voice mail. I went back into my contacts and tried his home number. He was one of the handful of people I knew who still had one.

His wife answered on the second ring.

"Angie, it's Danny. Can I talk to Paul?"

"Danny, he's sleeping. You should be too."

"Yeah, well… I had a sort of family emergency in California."

"Oh," she said, but still didn't offer to get Big Paul.

"Would you mind waking him up for me?" I asked without adding the words *important* or *urgent*. Angie was a smart lady. I was sure she understood. Which she did.

About thirty seconds later, Big Paul got on the line. "Hey, Dan," he said, his voice groggy. I wondered if he'd be conscious enough to remember our conversation.

"Sorry to wake you."

"It's all right. How are things down in SoCal?"

"My brother had a bad accident and really did a number on himself. They're not sure he's going to make it."

"Shit. I'm sorry to hear that."

"Look… if I was needed a bit longer down here, would that be okay?"

"Hey, family always comes first."

"I know, but I might be here a week or so… and I wanted to hear your thoughts before I said anything to the other guys."

"Whatever you need to do, you do. The guys will understand."

"Thanks, Paul. Get back to sleep. I'll check in with you later."

We hung up and I shut off the car. I couldn't believe I was doing it. I didn't want to be there, but this wasn't about what I wanted to do. Big Paul had said it right—it was what I needed to do.

I went back into the hospital and was let into the ICU. As I walked through the gauntlet of patients, I could already hear my non-comatose family members engaging in one of our favorite family traditions, an argument.

I heard Tina say, "It makes sense. Dad can move into Billy's place with him—"

"No," Mom said. "He has no idea how to take care of him—"

Dad added, "Tina's gonna hire a nurse that'll help me—"

Mom countered, "Tina's not in charge. Danny is."

Tina said, "Danny's gone."

"I don't care—" Mom froze mid-sentence as she saw me come around the curtain. Tina and Dad followed her eyes and looked to me. I'd definitely surprised them all.

"I wish I was," I said, "but I'm not."

None of them said anything, which was nice for a change. Before I could lay things out for them, Dr. Pettis appeared next to me.

"Excuse me," she said to us all. "You're disturbing the other patients. If you can't keep your voices down, you're going to need to leave the unit."

"It's okay," I said. "We're just working out a few things. We'll keep it down."

"And what have *we* worked out?" Tina asked.

"I'm staying," I said.

Mom's face and voice brightened as she said, "Oh Danny—"

I cut her off. "It's only for a week or so, but you all need to listen to me. If I'm staying and doing this, it also means we're doing things my way. No exceptions. And if any of you has a problem with that, then I'm out of here."

"Danny Boy," Dad said. "It doesn't have to be your way or the highway. I could—"

"No. Billy named me for whatever damned reason, and that means I'm in charge of everything." I looked at Tina. "Right?"

She nodded. "That's right." Her agreement with me helped to back Dad down.

Mom stood and came to me, pulling me into a tight embrace. "Danny, this is wonderful."

Of all the words I'd choose to describe this moment, I couldn't say *wonderful* was one of them.

I looked over her shoulder and down at Billy. I thought I saw a smirk on his face.

What the hell had I just agreed to do?

12

THE FOUR OF US DROVE separately to Billy's house. Mom in her Lexus, Tina in her Audi, Dad in his Vette, and me in my Outlander. Can you guess which one of us hadn't been bought a car by Billy? The one of us he owed a vehicle to. While Mom deserved the Lexus and more for all the crap she'd put up with from Billy over the years, Dad wasn't worthy of that Vette. Tina denied he'd purchased the Audi for her, but I didn't really believe it.

I followed Mom over to Billy's place, since I'd never been there and didn't even know the address. She drove up into the Norco Hills, where the homes were pricey. She pulled into the driveway of a pretty swanky two-story home that overlooked the other high-priced houses in the neighborhood. I pulled into the driveway. Tina and Dad parked on the street.

Examining the house as I climbed out of my car, I shook my head. Mom had told me the Prick had bought it for cash. It had since tripled in value. Life really was upside down. His house easily had a value of a million bucks or so, though he'd never done an honest day's work in his life. I busted my ass almost nightly, and yet I still rented an apartment I'd outgrown years ago.

"Okay," Tina said as we all went up the walkway. "They'll transport Billy here by eleven tomorrow morning. The visiting nurse is scheduled to be here at that time too."

"You've got it all worked out, don't you?" I asked.

"Would you prefer to do it all yourself?"

"You don't want to know what I'd really prefer."

We stood behind Mom as she unlocked Billy's front door and opened the house. A high-pitched beeping blared from the alarm system. Mom stepped inside and keyed the four-digit code on the alarm's wall panel. The beeping stopped.

Tina followed Mom in. My feet wouldn't move to allow me to enter.

Dad came up behind me. "You all right, Danny Boy?"

"Yeah," I lied, inhaled deeply, and crossed the threshold into the Prick's house.

The first thing that hit me was the smell. The lingering odor of tobacco, marijuana, rotten food, and who knew what else owned the air. Tina flipped on the entryway lights. They illuminated a place full of contradictions.

Billy had furnished the place with high-end products likely purchased at the Sharper Image or some store like that. Yet in typical Billy fashion, he'd let everything go to hell. Trash from fast food wrappers, discarded pizza boxes, and empty beer bottles covered everything. I couldn't even see the coffee table from all the debris on it. The mess included ashtrays that should've been dumped a month ago, at least one vape pen, a couple of pipes, and one visible bong.

"This place needs a surgeon general's warning," I said.

"When he's sober, it's spotless," Mom said, defending him as usual.

"At least it's been clean for about one week, then."

"Danny…"

I chose not to push it and add to Mom's stress. That would have been contrary to my purpose of staying. I stepped ahead and away from the others to give myself an unguided tour of the Prick's palatial pigsty.

The first door I came to off to the right was a bedroom. I turned on the light. Framed posters of the different Avengers movies hung from the walls. A single bed sat in the middle of the room. It had a bedspread from *The Force Awakens*.

It was the Kid's room.

I shut off the light, closed the door, and exited. There'd be no reason for me to go in there again.

Further into the house and to the right was another door. It went out to the garage. Flicking on the lights, I discovered it had been built to house three cars. There was only one car in this spacious garage, though—an orange Toyota Supra, just like Paul Walker's character drove in *The Fast and the Furious*.

I exited the garage and found Mom, Dad, and Tina gathered in a family room that also opened into the kitchen with a huge island.

"What was he driving?" I asked.

"What?" Tina responded.

"What kind of car was he driving when he crashed?"

Dad answered, "'70 Dodge Charger."

"Black?" I asked.

"Yeah," he said. "It was gorgeous."

Just like the one Vin Diesel drove in the first movie. It shouldn't have surprised me. Billy had always loved mindless action flicks with plenty of violence and car chases.

I went up the stairs that were built into the wall on the right. What disgusting and disturbing things awaited on the second story, I did not know. Still, I had an unexpected curiosity to discover.

The first room I came to was Billy's bedroom. It was a greater mess than anything downstairs. Piles of dirty clothes covered the floor. His bedsheets were twisted and balled up. Beer bottles, dirty glasses with extinguished cigarettes floating in whatever liquid they still held, and several orange bottles of pills occupied the nightstand.

I stepped over a mound of clothes to examine the pill bottles. They were a smorgasbord of the opioids that had become the drugs of choice across America in the last few years. Billy had Xanax, Vicodin, Percocet, and, of course, oxycodone. I saw the names of at least three different doctors listed on the various pill bottles. Can't say I was surprised. If you have the money, you can find a doctor to prescribe you just about anything. Ask Elvis, Michael Jackson, and Prince.

I shifted my attention away from Billy's collection of pill bottles and found myself facing a wall of photos I hadn't noticed when I'd entered the room. Naturally, they were of the Slut and the Kid. The pictures of the two, some framed and others taped to the plaster, covered the wall across from the closet. They'd been taken over the years. The framed ones were from back when the Kid had just been born. Another was of the three of them that could almost make you think they were one lovely little happy family.

The remainder of the pictures from the years revealed that the Slut had finally wised up. She wasn't in them, just the Kid. Some were of him with Billy. Most were just the Kid. School pictures, Little League pictures, soccer pictures. You could see his whole life over the last decade. I guessed he must be eleven now.

The Kid looked a lot like Billy. He had the Meacham nose and the Slut's eyes. He'd also inherited the butt chin that Billy and Dad had. Good. He deserved that stupid chin.

For some reason, I focused on the oldest picture hanging on the wall. It was of all three of them: the Prick, the Slut, and the Kid when he was an infant. I could feel Billy staring at me from the photo. He had that grin on his face, the same one he always had when he screwed me over. He spoke to me from the picture. I could hear him in my head.

That's right. I got her. You didn't.

13

As I HURRIED DOWN THE stairs, my instinct to keep going right out the front door to my car and back to Vegas kicked in. But I didn't. Instead, I turned right into the kitchen that opened into a family room. There I found Dad planted on a sofa in front of Billy's gigantic TV. A preseason Angels game was on. Dad had the volume turned up loud enough for the entire block to know the pitch count.

In the adjoining kitchen, Tina placed various bottles of liquor from the other counter inside a cardboard box that sat on the center island.

"There's nothing for you to worry about," Mom told Tina. "I haven't had a drink in over ten years."

"It's only some more trash we need to get rid of," Tina said, then looked to me. "Right?"

Great. Pull me right into the middle of this. I actually agreed with Tina about the booze. While Mom's sobriety had been unquestionable, it was best to remove the temptation, especially given the stress of the situation.

I replied by opening the fridge. Inside I found a bag of

rotting grapes, a white Styrofoam to-go container emitting a smell close to death, a half-full gallon of milk, likely spoiled, and a bottom shelf full of Billy's favorite soft drink: Bud Light.

"You might want to clear out some of this garbage, too," I said to Tina.

Tina saw the beer and nodded. "I will."

"I can't believe you two don't believe me when I tell you I have absolutely no urge to drink," Mom said.

"I believe you," Tina said. "I'd just like to keep it that way." Tina moved over to the refrigerator with a bag to grab the beer. "Oh my goodness, this is gross."

"Can't say that it's not," I said as I moved away, crossing the living room to the sliding glass doors. Outside, an incredible walk-in infinity pool shimmered under the early afternoon sun. It blended into the horizon. It provided a view that would've been incredible if it weren't for the two freeways crisscrossing one another, plus the light cushion of smog that hung over everything.

The blaring sound of the Angels game suddenly ended.

"Why'd you do that?" Dad said.

I turned to find Mom with the remote in hand, standing beside Dad and the sofa. "We're not here for you to watch baseball," Mom said. "We're here to get this place cleaned up so Billy can come home."

Even though the years and their marriage had passed, it seemed like I'd just stepped back in time to my parents' living room twenty years ago or so.

"I was just checking the score," Dad said.

"Then I'm sure you've seen it," Mom said.

Dad jumped to his feet. "The Halos had a runner on third!"

"If you want to watch the game, you can go home and watch the game."

"But I'm here now."

I'd had enough. "Are you two really going to do this?"

My parents both looked at me as if I was the one with the problem.

"She's the one who turned off the TV," Dad said, pointing at Mom.

"Because we're not here for you to watch baseball," Mom repeated to him.

"I told you, I was just checking the score!" Dad said.

"Dad," I said. "It's preseason. It doesn't matter."

Dad mulled it over then said. "You're right. And until they get rid of Sciossa, it probably won't."

It wasn't wholly the concession I'd been looking for, but it was good enough.

Tina came into the family room with us, checking her watch for nothing more than effect. "Before we all know it, Billy's going to be here, and there's a lot of work to get done. Mom, why don't you and Danny start in the living room? Dad and I can get to work upstairs."

"Sounds fine to me," I said, having no desire to be in Billy's bedroom with those pictures, touch his sheets, or, God forbid, pick up his underwear.

Mom agreed by heading over into the living room, but Dad seemed lost by it all. Tina noticed it too and said to him, "Come on, Dad."

Dad stood up to go upstairs with Tina. She had defused the situation quite effectively.

Or so I thought until Dad said, "Anyone mind if I have the game on so I can listen to it?"

"I saw a TV upstairs, but keep the volume very low," I told him, wondering how Mom had stayed married to him as long as she had.

14

By SUNSET, BILLY'S HOUSE HAD reached a somewhat livable condition. It really wasn't that hard to achieve. Several weeks of trash, dirty dishes, unwashed clothes, and ash from various things that had been smoked needed to be dealt with. It takes far less time if you take care of such things on a regular basis every few days. Or he could have hired a cleaning service to come in weekly to keep his place in order. That would make practical and common sense. The Prick, however, lacked both.

The upstairs carpets still needed vacuuming and the bathrooms scrubbing, but having been awake for a little over twenty-four hours, I didn't have the energy to keep going. The others hadn't even lasted as long as I had.

Dad had proven mostly useless. Once the Angels game was over, he started complaining of a hernia he needed surgery for but couldn't afford because he wasn't on Medicare yet. Tina was the next to take the opportunity to bolt. She was in the middle of prepping for a trial and needed to get to work on that. Mom had to stop and catch her breath about every five minutes or so.

When I came in from dropping a bulging Hefty bag next to the also overflowing garbage cans out by the street, Mom was waiting for me by the door. She studied me for a moment then said, "You look tired."

"Yeah, I didn't get any sleep last night."

"You can come stay in your room tonight if you want."

"That sounds great."

Tina had washed Billy's sheets and made the bed, but I didn't feel like staying in his house. Not yet, anyway. I'd need to get over that, but it could wait at least a day.

I rode shotgun with Mom as she drove to her house. She didn't take the same route out that we came in. She cut through back streets that ran between the other houses of this community then came down behind the high school.

Norco High didn't look like the same place in reality that I saw in my memories. It was bigger. Lots more buildings. The football field where I'd graduated had changed too. They'd finally replaced those decrepit wooden bleachers with professional-looking stands and a nice-looking playing field. They even had a new scoreboard, but it was on the opposite end of the field from where it was back when. My little high school had grown up.

Fortunately, the town hadn't changed all that much, at least not on the residential streets. The horse trails were still there and sidewalks had yet to crop up. Despite the crush of building around the city and on its main streets, Norco hadn't given in to the pressure to citify itself. How long could it hold out? I didn't know. But it was nice to see that the town I'd grown up in had done its best to retain its country charm.

If it hadn't been for Norco, I probably never would have been exposed to country music. Dad hated it and refused to give up on rock and roll. But country had gotten a hold of me at a pretty young age. Garth Brooks hit when I was eight and more or less dominated country throughout my teenage years. The '90s were a great time for country music. To Dad's never-ending chagrin, I learned every one of the hit songs. As much as he'd disappointed me, it was the least I could do in return.

Coming off of Hillside, Mom turned left at Sixth Street. The first things I noticed were that the lines on Sixth were still painted red, white, and blue. The city had done that after 9/11 as a sign of patriotism and had kept it that way.

Mom hit the blinker to turn right onto Center Street. I looked over at the opposite corner and saw the Circle K. Billy had had his first car accident there when I was seventeen. Further up Center—a block away, actually— he'd had his most recent one. I found it interesting that they'd all happened more or less on the same street, but tried not to dwell on it too much. Elton John's "Circle of Life" played in my head once again.

Mom pulled into the driveway of her house. The

house I'd grown up in. The one place that—despite all the chaos that had emanated out of it—I would probably always consider home.

I got out and looked down at the pavement. All of our initials—TM, DM, and BM—were etched into the cement. Every time I looked at that spot, my two upper front teeth seemed to throb. It had to be in my mind because there was no way I could still feel them break after all these years.

As we walked up to the front door, Mom said, "I'm not really up for cooking. How's pizza sound?"

"Pepperoni and black olive?" When it had been my turn to pick the toppings on Pizza Night, those were always the ones I ordered.

Mom smiled. "Of course."

Her house hadn't changed much either over the years, except it smelled better. Being forced to give up the habit of half a pack of Marlboro 100's per day had made a better impact than a Living Air ever did. She needed to replace the carpet and maybe get the place painted, but just as it did whenever I visited, this still felt like the home I'd grown up in.

I intentionally ignored the wall in the family room that was covered with family pictures, most of them from when we were kids. There were plenty of me, Tina, and Billy. All of the photos of Dad in any capacity had been removed after Mom kicked him out, starting with their Las Vegas wedding photo. Pictures of the Kid had gone up on their place. I wished they weren't there, but there wasn't anything I could do about that here. This was Mom's house. The wall of photos in Billy's bedroom was a different story.

I grabbed a shower, and when I got out, Domino's had delivered our dinner. Mom and I sat down at the dining room table and ate.

"So," Mom said as she finished her second slice, "have you been seeing anyone?"

I should have known the question was coming. It always did. "I see lots of people."

"Anyone seriously?"

"No one worth bringing down for an interrogation."

"Don't you ever think about getting married?"

Uh-oh. Mom was pushing hard. I needed to get out of this.

"With all that's going on right now, is that really important?" I asked.

"Your happiness is always important to me."

"And marriage was the key to your happiness?"

"Your father and I were a different story. Back then, a girl got married if she got pregnant. Even if it only happened because she'd been out looking for a little fun."

"Whoa, Mom. TMI."

"What's that mean?"

"It means you don't talk about things like that to your son."

"Well, how do you think any of you got here if your

father and I weren't having sex?"

"I get that it had to happen. I just don't want to hear about *how* it happened."

"It's not exactly a fond memory of mine either. If I hadn't been drinking back then, I doubt I would've even let him get to second base."

I pushed back from the table. "Mom! Really?"

"What? Was that TMY too?"

I stood up and took my plate to the kitchen sink. "T-M-I," I said. "And yes, that's pretty much the definition of it."

"Well, I'm sorry if I offended your sensibilities."

"Look, I'm exhausted. I really need to get some sleep."

"Well, you know where your room is."

I came back over to the table, leaned down and kissed her cheek. Then I headed down the hall to what was once my bedroom for what I intended to be a long, deep, much-needed night of sleep.

I wasn't sure what tomorrow held in store, but I knew it would be a big day, one way or the other.

PART II

My Brother's Keeper

1

THE MOVIES ARE FULL OF crap.

They make it appear that roosters crow to announce the sunrise. Nope. They start much earlier than dawn. That's a fact you learn early in life when you grow up in an animal-keeping town like Norco.

I heard the first cock-a-doodle-doo around three a.m.

Dammit. I hadn't slept at all.

Despite being up for more than an entire day, I couldn't sleep that night. Maybe it was being back home. Maybe it was my nighttime work and daytime sleep schedule. Maybe it was this crap Billy had dropped upon me. Or maybe it was the lack of sex this weekend. Yeah, that was probably it.

I couldn't remember the last weekend I hadn't been laid at least once. No, wait. I could. It was that tour with the third main iteration of my band, The Regulators. I'd foolishly believed there was someone waiting for me worth being faithful to. While my bandmates scored after pretty much every show in every state and town we played, I dedicated myself to reading. Yeah, I was young and naïve back then.

Lying there in my old bed, I thought about rubbing one out. Taking the edge off would probably allow me to snooze. Despite having jerked off countless nights in this very room when I was a teenager, I resisted. I hadn't had to provide myself with my own sexual gratification in years. That wasn't a streak I felt like breaking.

My thoughts scurried all over the place. I wondered about the guys and how our gig had gone. Rusty had talent, so I knew he'd do good, but would the dynamic of only a quartet work? I liked the sound we made by having two guitars. Only having one would leave something lacking, but I'd be back soon enough.

If Tina was right—and according to her, she always was—Billy only needed a week or so to recover. I calculated "or so" to equal ten days. I'd give the Prick ten days. For Mom's sake, at the very least. But would he recover? I had my doubts about that, even if no one else in the family did. It seemed evident to me from the doctor's briefing that Billy had mashed his little brain pretty good in that crash.

Still, he'd survived a lot of crazy "accidents" over the years. In the third grade, he did a backward flip off the swings that was strictly against the playground rules. He could've broken his neck. He only broke his wrist.

In junior high, he went dirt bike riding in the hills, deciding that helmets were for sissies. When he went down, he scraped off the left side of his face, but somehow didn't do any lasting damage.

The same was true when he stole my car and rolled it on Sixth Street when we were in high school. For some reason, the dipshit buckled up during his quick trip to Circle K for some dip, and didn't splatter his brains all over pavement.

My favorite of his accidents really should've killed him. I wasn't present but was still living at home, so I saw the aftermath.

Billy and some of his loser friends had gone to a concert at the old Universal Amphitheater. After the show, the genius had the idea to dive off a bridge in the amusement park into what looked like a flowing river. But Hollywood's all about optical illusions, and that "river" turned out to be a very shallow stream. He didn't quite walk away from that one, but, miracles of miracles, he didn't wind up dead or a quadriplegic.

Any of those things or the variety of car accidents he'd been in over the years easily could have killed the Prick. He'd be long since buried up at Crestlawn and no longer a thorn in my ass. But no such luck. Even though Billy never landed on his feet like a cat, he seemed to possess a feline's alleged nine lives.

Maybe he'd make it through this one.

In a few days, he'd stir and take a disoriented look around. When he did, the Prick would see me sitting there. It would prove that he'd named me his agent simply to screw up my current state of life.

But I'd prove something to him too.
That would be the day, wouldn't it?
Yes. Yes, it would be.
I liked that idea. I liked it a lot.

2

THE HOSPITAL BED TINA ORDERED arrived slightly before ten a.m. It had a rocking mechanism built into it, so I wouldn't have to turn him to prevent bedsores. That was more than fine with me. So was the premium fee Tina had to pay for rushed delivery. It was the Prick's money, not my own.

Tina had gotten to Billy's house as I was setting up the bed with a small bit of assistance from Mom. My sister had taken the morning off from work, as she didn't need to be in court until the afternoon. That gave her the time required to attempt to supervise me. I wished she'd just gone to work. But at least she helped me get the bed in working order before the ambulance arrived a few minutes after eleven.

Following mutual hellos and such, two young paramedics wheeled Billy and the machines I'd seen him hooked up to in the hospital into the living room. I'd pushed all of the furniture up against the walls. This area would be serving as Billy's room. With an impressive combination of professional care and skill, the paramedics effortlessly transferred the Prick from the gurney to his new bed.

I stared at the numerous tubes sticking out of the machines and into him.

Billy shouldn't be here.

He belongs in some type of home where they can take care of him appropriately. Not here. And not with me.

Mom had to see this now.

Nope. While she still looked concerned, Mom seemed more peaceful than at any point in the hospital yesterday.

"Could you sign this please?" one of the paramedics asked, handing me a pad and a stylus. Without saying a word, I signed the screen. "Thank you, Mr. Meacham," he said. "Now, do you have someone that's going to be helping you out here?"

"I thought I did."

I turned to Tina. Finally, one of her plans hadn't worked out.

"What happened to this visiting nurse you said you hired?" I asked my sister.

"She got stuck in traffic on the 91," the answer came, but not from Tina. The female voice had come from behind me.

In the frame of the still-open front door stood an incredibly beautiful woman. She had tan skin and long, wavy black hair loosely tied back in a ponytail. She wore blue scrubs that I found oddly arousing. I'd never been a fan of scrubs, but on this nurse they seemed to bring out the contours of what must've been an exceptional body.

I slyly glanced down at her left hand, which gripped a small black canvas bag. No ring. Maybe that was an occupational thing. I checked her right, where she held the strap of a small cooler. She did have a ring on her middle right finger. Hmm. A sexy nurse without a husband or fiancé that would be coming here five days a week. I was confident I'd just found my next project.

Maybe Billy didn't need to be put in a home after all.

At least not right away.

"I'm sorry for being late," Project Nurse said as she came over to us.

"Being on time for your first day is overrated," I said. "If you want to stand out, being a little late will do the trick."

She smiled and maintained strong eye contact with me. "I'll have to keep that in mind."

"You should."

"I'm guessing you're Mr. Meacham."

"Oh, no. That's the guy I have to call Dad. I'm Danny."

She offered her hand. "Veronica Becerra."

I took it, giving it a light shake. She had a strong hand but soft skin. I instantly imagined how good the rest of her skin would feel against mine.

Mom stepped over and took Veronica's hand from mine. "I'm Carol. And this is my daughter Tina."

"It's nice to meet you both," Veronica said.

Tina, uncharacteristically, didn't say a word. I noticed the muscles in her face had tightened. She watched Veronica with glaring eyes. Chicks, man.

Veronica must've picked up on Tina's vibe, and said to her, "I really do apologize for my tardiness. I'll be sure to leave earlier from now on."

"Oh, the 91 is the worst freeway in the state," Mom said. "The important thing is that you're here now to help take care of Billy."

And hopefully me, too.

Mom, still holding Veronica's hand, led her over to Billy's bed.

Veronica looked down at her patient and asked, "How you doing, Billy?"

He didn't reply. That's a major side effect of a coma.

"Does it help to talk to him?" Mom asked Veronica.

"Many comatose patients who've awakened said they heard everything that was spoken to them," Veronica said.

Mom allowed herself a slight smile. "I talk to him all the time."

Tina continued to watch Veronica with suspicious eyes then announced to us all, "Well, I need to get to the office."

"It's nice to meet you," Veronica said.

Tina ignored Veronica and said to Mom, "I'll be back this evening. Please let me know if anything happens."

"Of course I will," Mom said.

Tina pivoted and walked to the door. As she passed

me, she whispered, "A quick word with you, little brother?"

"Sure," I said much louder than a whisper.

"Outside," Tina said through gritted teeth.

I didn't know or care what my sister wanted to tell me or what had set her off. I only wanted to get her on the road so I could get to work on my new project. To speed Tina along, I went out front with her.

3

"I'M CALLING THE SERVICE ON the way in and having them replace her," Tina said as soon as we were outside and she'd shut the door behind us.

"For being five minutes late?"

"Don't be obtuse. I saw you two flirting."

"I was being friendly," I said.

"Look, you're here to take care of Billy."

"Which I don't know the first thing about, and which is why she's here, right?"

"She still needs to be replaced."

"You're the one who found her."

"I found the service. I didn't know they'd send *her*."

"Well, they did, and I can't say I'm complaining."

"She's already a distraction."

"No, she's not."

"Danny, I saw the way you were looking at her. You totally want to hump her."

"Now there's a word I haven't heard since the fourth grade," I said, unable to suppress a chuckle.

"Don't try to change the subject. Your top priority

needs to be Billy."

"It is."

"Is it?"

"I assure you that of all the things I plan to do today, the nurse is third on the list."

That quip got right under Tina's skin, as I'd intended. "I'm serious."

"So am I. Have you taken a look into Billy's shower? The cure for Ebola could be growing in there with who the hell knows what else."

Tina turned to leave and said, "I'm calling the service on the way to work and having them send over another nurse."

"Oh no, you're not." My words stopped her. "I'm Billy's agent, remember? I make all decisions. So while you may have found her, I technically hired her. And since I'm in charge, I say she stays."

"Danny, please—"

"It's not open for debate."

That did little to calm Tina down. She wanted to argue the point. I wasn't going to let her. She wasn't getting between Project Nurse and me.

"Shouldn't you be getting to work?" I asked. "Taking too much time off could really screw up your chance of getting that promotion."

Tina's face tightened. She knew I wasn't budging. "We'll talk about this later."

"No. I don't think we will."

I turned my back on my sister, went inside, and closed the door before I could hear any more of her complaints or protests. I put an artificial smile on my face as I approached Project Nurse, who still stood at the bed with Mom.

"Everything all right?" Mom asked me.

"Tina just wanted to give me a little pep talk."

Mom's look said she knew I'd lied, but she let it drop. I looked over to Project Nurse as she unpacked the bag she'd carried in.

"All ready to get started?" Veronica asked.

"Absolutely. Make yourself at home and do whatever you need to do. If you need me for anything, I'll be upstairs doing a full biohazard decontamination on a shower."

"Umm... that's not quite how this works," Veronica said. "Your brother needs around-the-clock care."

"Right. That's why I hired you."

"I'm only here during the day and that's only five days a week. The rest of the time, everything falls on his primary caregiver. Which I believe is you."

Wait a minute. Hold the phone.

"No one said anything about that," I said.

"It's often more than most people expect, but after a day or two, you'll get the hang of it."

"Are you saying I can't leave here?"

"Oh, no. Not at all. It's just that someone does need to be here with him at all times, and there's a lot I need to show you today."

No. I wasn't going to let Billy trap me here like this. Granted, I'd be trapped here with an amazing project, but virtual house arrest with his invalid ass wasn't what I'd signed up for.

"But I've got a lot of other things to do today," I said. "I mean, there's absolutely zero food in this place."

"I don't mind going to the store for you," Mom said.

What was Mom doing? I couldn't be stuck here alone with Billy.

I looked over at Veronica and quickly hit pause on that line of thought. Where was my brain? If Mom went to get groceries... yes, I'd be stuck there with Billy, but... I'd also be stuck there with Project Nurse... and without any other conscious family members around for a while.

"All right. Thanks, Mom. I appreciate it," I said. "Can you pick me up some Diet Dr. Pepper and some Cheez-Its?"

"Healthy diet you have there," Veronica said.

Damn.

Probably not a great move to let a medical professional know you don't follow any serious nutritional guidelines in your life. Fortunately, Mom helped cover for me.

"I'll get you plenty of fruit, too. And I'll pick up all the ingredients to make you some meatloaf this week," Mom said as she grabbed her purse and headed for the door with her oxygen machine.

"Yeah," I said. "That sounds great."

"Call me if anything happens," Mom said, heading out

the door.

"Will do," I said, knowing that some explicit details wouldn't be recounted later to my mother.

Once Mom was out the door, I turned my full attention back to Project Nurse and gave her my best panty-dropper smile.

"So, where do we start?" I asked.

She pulled a pair of latex gloves from her bag. "Let's get gloved up," she said.

Oh…

I liked the way things were going.

4

"BESIDES PNEUMONIA, THE BIGGEST RISKS Billy faces are blood clots and infections," Veronica said as she popped a needle into the rubber top of a medicine bottle and pulled the plunger back with her latex-gloved hands.

I wore the pair she'd given me. She'd sent me into the bathroom to wash my hands thoroughly. I'd scrubbed them good like all those actors playing surgeons on TV shows I'd seen throughout the years. I was surprised to find how tight the gloves fit. There was a weird, powdery feel to them.

When the syringe had filled with fluid, Veronica said, "Your brother has to have his antibiotics twice a day and the blood thinner once."

She pulled the needle out of the bottle then offered the syringe to me. I took a step back. I'd never been a fan of needles. Even though that one wasn't intended for me, I still didn't want to be too close to it. Veronica stared at me, waiting for me to take it from her.

"As much as I would enjoy sticking it to him," I said, "I'm going to leave this to you."

"There's nothing to it," she said, "'cause you're not

really giving him a shot."

Veronica found a tube sticking out of Billy's right arm that didn't connect to anything. She put the needle into the opening in the tube, then pressed the top of the syringe down. That shot its contents into the tube and up into Billy's arm.

"You're pretty good at that," I said, hoping to recover some coolness I might've lost.

"I've had a lot of practice with needles."

"Then I guess you've been doing this a long time."

"No, I'm pretty new. But I did have a pretty heavy heroin habit for a while."

Whoa.

I hadn't expected that and wasn't sure what to think. I'd heard plenty of nurses became hooked on the drugs they were giving their patients. Was she an addict? If so, she could scratch her ass off the project list, regardless how sexy that ass might be.

Veronica smiled and gave a little laugh. The look on my face must've conveyed the concerning thoughts that had raced through my mind.

"I'm joking," she said. Her words made me feel both stupid and relaxed at the same time. I stared down at the carpet we'd vacuumed yesterday. "I've been an RN for nine years now, and doing home health care for about six of them."

I looked back up at her, needing to get back in the conversation. "You prefer this to working in a hospital?"

"Yes and no. The schedule's better, and this job does allow me to get closer with my patients... but that also makes the losses a lot harder."

I gestured a gloved hand down toward Billy. "Well, in this condition, you probably don't have to worry about forming too much of a bond with him."

"You might be surprised."

Hmm. Interesting.

"Let me ask you something," I said.

"Sure."

I paused. I wanted to know, or at least I thought I did, but for some reason that I didn't understand, I had a hard time getting the words to come out of my mouth.

"Given your experience," I finally said, "what's the chances that he'll wake up and snap out of this?"

Veronica stared down at Billy for a long moment. He didn't move, of course. Maybe she was trying to pick up some vibration of any brain waves he might have. After a few more seconds, she brought her eyes up to mine and gave me her opinion.

5

"IT'S HARD TO TELL," VERONICA said. "The brain is incredibly complex, and head trauma's a tricky thing. Each person's different. It's more or less a wait-and-see type thing."

"So I've been told."

It frustrated me that no one could provide me with a straight answer about Billy's odds of coming out of this or how banged up his pea-sized brain might truly be.

"On a positive note," Veronica said, "you did the right thing by bringing him home."

"Can't say I'm so sure about that."

"Your brother has a much better chance of recovering here than if he were in a nursing facility."

"They really that bad?"

"There's a reason we call them vegetable patches."

Yikes.

"Do me a favor," I said. "Under no circumstances ever mention that in front of my mom."

I didn't need Mom knowing that term and using it against me if a "vegetable patch" was where I needed to send Billy in the near future.

"I'll be careful around her," Veronica said as she went to her mini cooler and took a blue and white bottle of Ensure from it.

"You drink that stuff?" I asked. "I thought it was for old people."

"I do, but it isn't for me. It's full of nutrients that Billy's body needs, especially protein. So on top of the meals we're going to be providing, we need to give him one of these each day."

Veronica screwed the top off the Ensure and grabbed a giant syringe out of her bag. She stuck it into the Ensure and pulled the plunger back, filling it with white liquid.

"You're just gonna shoot him up with that?" I asked.

"Actually, you're going to." Veronica pulled Billy's hospital gown up, revealing the plastic tube they'd put into him at Loma Linda. "First, you need to open the valve."

I took a step forward, pretending this didn't freak me out, and turned the valve stem open. Some disgusting kind of yellow liquid squirted up into the tube. I jumped back.

"What the hell?" I said.

"They're gastric juices. That's a good thing."

"It is?"

"It means the feeding tube's actually in his stomach."

Veronica grabbed the top of the tube and shoved the giant syringe into it. Then she offered it to me. I took a tentative step forward and took it from her.

"Now," she said, "depress the plunger and give your

brother his lunch."

I did as instructed. As I pressed the plunger into the syringe, the milky liquid flooded into the feeding tube, filling it up and pushing the gastric juice back into Billy's stomach. I kept my eyes on the syringe and continued to push it down at a steady rate. That's when Veronica decided to get chatty.

"So, Danny, don't call me Mr. Meacham—you a local boy?"

"Born and raised right here in good ole' Horsetown U.S.A."

"Still here, huh?"

"I come to visit now and then," I said, avoiding specifics. "I live up in a little town north of here you might've heard of called Las Vegas."

"What happens there allegedly stays there."

"At least it did before everyone had video cameras on their phones."

I liked that she wanted to flirt. I suppose our little back-and-forth excited her too. She reached out and put her gloved hand on mine.

"Slow down," she said. "You don't want to give him too much too fast."

I did as she said and looked up at her. She didn't look away. I didn't expect that she would. Confident women don't look away. They know what they want and go right for it.

She broke the silence, saying, "You don't strike me as a

dealer or a pit boss."

"That's old Las Vegas. You don't have to have greasy hair or a flat forehead to get a job in a casino now."

"Mmm... I still don't see it."

"Maybe I'm a professional gambler."

"Naw. You've got too many tells for that."

"I do?"

"Tons."

"Hence why I never gamble."

"Then how do you make your living?"

"I entertain people," I said, baiting the hook.

"Care to elaborate?"

"I don't usually talk about that with someone I just met."

"Depending on how things go with Billy, you and I could wind up spending a lot of time together."

That wasn't a nibble. That was a big honking bite.

"In that case," I said, "I probably should let you know that, well... I'm an exotic dancer."

"Oh, really?" Her face didn't give away whether she believed me or not.

"Yep. I get paid to shake this money maker."

I gave a pelvic swivel and thrust that would've made Elvis proud.

She smiled. "You do that very well."

"Give me twenty dollars and I'll show you my whole routine."

"I mean the confidence thing. You pull it off without

coming off too arrogant."

Huh?

I hadn't seen that coming.

"I'm not sure if that's a compliment or not." I honestly didn't.

"Take it as one."

"Then thanks, I guess."

"You're welcome," Veronica said. "And I know I'm probably going to burst your bubble here, but that's about all you're going to get from me."

6

WAIT. WHAT THE HELL JUST HAPPENED?

I'd had Project Nurse on the hook. I'd been reeling her in steadily.

Did she really think she was going to break my line and swim off?

"I don't even know what you're talking about," I said.

"When you went outside to talk with your sister, your mom asked me if I was single and happened to mention that you were too."

Of course she had. "Thanks, Mom."

"She said it with the best of intentions."

"I'm sure she did. But I'm taking that means you're not single."

"Oh, I'm completely unattached."

Okay. I can still land this one. Just need to bring her in with more finesse.

I looked Veronica straight in the eye and said, "I hope that doesn't make things too awkward between us."

"It shouldn't."

"Good."

"Because I have a rule that I never become involved with someone I work for. It helps make things clearer and easier on the job."

Seriously?

Was Project Nurse going to make me the victim of my own "no hooking up with the people you work with" rule?

No. No, she wasn't.

I took a shot at her. Looking at the Prick, I said, "Even if he was awake, I can't say that Billy would be your type."

She looked down at him, giving the Prick a solid once-over. "That's too bad. He's quite cute." Then she looked up at me. "But I wasn't talking about him. You're the one who hired me."

"Technically, my sister did that."

"Wasn't that on your behalf?"

"It's kinda convoluted, so maybe you should consider a one-time exception to your rule."

"Bending the rules is how people get into trouble."

"Or into fun."

"The trouble always seems to last longer than the fun does."

Project Nurse wasn't caving. Neither was I. Her persistence actually turned me on.

"I could always fire you, and then we could go out," I said.

"But then I'd resent you and wouldn't want anything to do with you."

Damn.

She wasn't moving off her rule even half an inch. I figured a more direct approach might work.

"So either way, I'm screwed."

"Or not, as the case may be."

That was a nice comeback. I couldn't tell if Veronica was being nice yet firm or playing hard to get.

I noticed the Ensure from the syringe was all inside Billy now.

"Well," I said as I lifted the syringe, "everything's looking about half-empty around here now."

"Don't pout. There are plenty of things we can still do together."

Excellent, Smithers. She still wanted to flirt.

"Oh yeah?" I said, trying to sound optimistic but not gleeful.

"Mmm-hmmm," Veronica said, and again took my gloved right hand in hers.

She held my eyes at the same time she held my head.

Oh yeah. Project Nurse was majorly into me.

Her rule must have a few nuances to it that she wanted me to work to discover.

"This is probably going to be a new experience for you," she said.

"I like new experiences."

"I thought you might."

Gently, Veronica moved my hand in hers up under Billy's hospital gown. Her eyes never broke contact with mine.

"Let me show you have to change his catheter," Veronica said she as rested my hand on top of Billy's shaft.

I recoiled and yanked my hand away from Billy's crank and out of Veronica's. "Whoa!" I said, jumping away. "Isn't this what I'm paying you for?"

She smiled at me, clearly pleased that she could rattle me.

"You seemed concerned that I might get too close to your brother."

"If that's how you want to be close to him, then be my guest."

"I told you, I'm not going to be here all the time."

"Well, you can do *this* when you are."

"It's not like you're fondling him. You're changing his catheter. It's no different than taking a condom off. I'm sure you've done that a time or two, Mr. Exotic Dancer."

"Not off another guy."

"You're wearing gloves."

"Doesn't matter."

"Don't be such a wuss. He's your brother."

"We're really not that close."

"Then let me help you both get a lot closer."

Veronica grabbed my hand and again moved it up between Billy's legs. She had my fingers on to the end of the catheter sleeve that covered the Prick's prick.

"Now pull it off, but do it slowly," she said.

I closed my eyes as I did so, not wanting to be there.

True, Billy and I had seen each other naked plenty when we were little kids. Mom even bathed us together. I'm pretty sure she had a picture of that some place. But that was a long time ago, and I never touched his wee-wee.

My entire life, I'd only held on to one penis. The one attached to me. Having another man's junk between my fingers, especially Billy's, wasn't right. There was no part of this that wasn't wrong in the wrongest way.

The sound of the front door opening and the alarm beeping pulled me back into the room. Mom's return from the store couldn't have had better timing. But it wasn't Mom who spoke.

"Hey there, Danny Boy!"

The sound of Dad's voice untethered the last part of my self-control I'd held on to. I lurched back and pulled the rest of the catheter off too fast. I instantly felt warm liquid on my face and neck. With one whiff, I recognized the odor. I opened my eyes. Billy's urine dripped down from my head on to my shirt.

Veronica attempted to stifle her laugh, but failed.

Dad gave me a once-over and smirked.

"Now that's a helluva way to bond with your brother."

7

HOW'S THAT FOR A METAPHOR come to life?

Billy had been pissing all over me in a figurative sense for as long as I could remember. Now the Prick had done it literally. And right in front of Project Nurse. Proof yet again that, conscious or comatose, Billy always found a way to screw with me.

To make the matter worse, Dad was now throwing what he considered charm at Veronica. As I headed up the stairs to change, Dad had already moved in on her.

"Well, hello there, and who might you be?" I heard him say to her.

"I'm Veronica. I'm Billy's nurse."

"And I'm his father, James."

"It's a pleasure to meet you, Mr. Meacham."

"Mr. Meacham? That's what I had to call that SOB of a father of mine. Call me James."

No!

Had Dad really used nearly the same line on her that I did?

I had to get back down there before he weirded her

out so much that she wouldn't want anything to do with me.

And I needed to stop using that "don't call me Mr. Meacham" line immediately.

I pulled the urine-damp shirt carefully over my head and off my body, doing all I could to avoid getting any more of Billy's piss on my face. I threw the soiled shirt on the floor and went to the bathroom, where I tossed the latex gloves in the trash and washed my face.

Opening up Billy's closet, I searched for a replacement shirt to wear. Since I'd had the strongest of intentions to only be down here a day or so, I'd only packed one shirt for the trip. I'd have to put on one of his now.

Everything hanging in the Prick's closet looked like it would fit me, but none of it was my style. Billy had tried to retain a young and hip fashion sense with the brands teenagers and twenty-somethings were wearing today. It made sense. He was a perpetual adolescent punk.

Other than a dark grey suit, his closet was full of shirts from Famous Stars & Straps, DC, and DGK-branded shirts. Nothing I'd ever worn, nor would I consider wearing if he hadn't pissed on my last clean shirt. The DC was the most normal of the ones there, so I chose it.

I came back downstairs to find Veronica next to Billy's bed. Dad stood as close to her as he could without dry-humping her leg like a hard-up springer spaniel.

"February twentieth," Dad said. "You just had your birthday."

"Yes, I did," she said.

"And was it a good birthday?"

"It was quite nice."

"So, February twentieth," Dad said. "What's that make you? An Aquarius?"

"Pisces."

"What an incredible coincidence."

"You're a Pisces too?"

"No, I'm a Taurus. But Tauruses and Pisces tend to have incredible chemistry."

"I don't know much about astrology," she said. "I always thought it was a bit of a joke."

That was a nice parry by Veronica to push Dad back. Yet he pressed on.

"I don't believe it can predict the future. If it could, I'd be in the Rock and Roll Hall of Fame. But it does reveal a lot about personalities and the way they interact."

Ugh. A hard-up Springer Spaniel would've had more restraint.

Reaching the bottom of the stairs, I decided to rescue Veronica.

"Dad," I said, "Can I have a word with you?"

"Sure, give me a minute," he said, waving me off.

"No. Kitchen. Now."

Dad looked at me. I thought he was going to protest, but he must've seen I was serious.

"If you'll excuse me for a moment," he said to Veronica, then followed me into the kitchen.

Before I could say anything, he leaned near to me as if to let me in on a secret, but he spoke at a volume louder than a horrible attempt at a whisper.

"I'll tell you, I've seen a lot of foxy women in my day, but that nurse is a total knockout."

"Her name is Veronica," I said in a much quieter tone.

"I've always loved that name."

"Dad... she's younger than me."

"I've scored with plenty of younger women. And quite recently, too."

What was with my parents lately? "TMI, Dad."

"What?"

"Don't go popping your Viagra just yet."

"Hey! I don't need any pills to raise the wood."

"I'm sure you can," I said more quietly, hoping he'd lower his voice too. "But she doesn't date people she works for. So chill out, okay?"

Dad took that in, seemed to weigh it over, then grinned at me.

I knew that grin. I'd seen it plenty of times, but not from my father. I'd seen it from Billy whenever he intended to do something contrary to my wishes.

"You're jealous," he said.

"What?"

"Yeah, you are. You're jealous I'm gonna get that tail and you're not."

"That's completely ridiculous."

"She ain't giving you any 'cause she works for you, but

I ain't got that problem, 'cause she don't work for me."

Dad straightened his collar, ran his fingers through his thinning but lengthy hair, and went back into the living room.

What the hell was his problem? Did he actually believe Veronica would want anything to do with him in the physical sense?

She was my project, dammit. Not his.

8

THIS TIME, VERONICA WAS FORTUNATE enough to be saved by the bell.

Actually, by the beeps.

When I stepped back into the living room to run interference for her against the pickup patheticness from my aging excuse of a father, the front door opened. The security system emitted its high-pitched triple beep. Seconds later, Mom and her strapped-on oxygen device came through the door carrying a white paper takeout bag.

"I'm back," Mom said.

The takeout bag confused me. "I thought you went to get groceries?" I asked.

"They're in my trunk. But when I was leaving Stater's, I realized it was close to lunchtime, so I went over to Sixth Street Deli and picked up some sandwiches."

"Perfect," Dad said. "I'm starved."

"I didn't get you one," Mom said then asked me. "When was the last time you had a hot pastrami from Sixth Street Deli?"

"Too damn long," I said.

"Well, your wait is over," she said, then looked to Veronica. "I picked up one for you too."

"That's very kind, but I packed my lunch," Veronica said, but Mom wasn't letting her off the hook that easily.

"Have you ever had a sandwich from Sixth Street Deli?" Mom asked.

"No, but—"

"You have no idea what you're missing," Mom said.

"You certainly don't," I chimed in.

"I do appreciate it," Veronica said, "but I'm fine."

"I'll eat it," Dad said.

Mom continued to ignore him and said to Veronica, "I'll put it in the fridge. You can heat it up later."

"Really, it's all right," Veronica said. "I'm training for a marathon and am on a pretty regimented diet."

"I said I'll take it," Dad said louder than before.

Mom finally answered him. "If you want a sandwich, you can go and buy one,"

"Why can't I just have that one?"

"Because it's not for you."

Their exchange clearly made Veronica feel uncomfortable, so she tried to defuse it. Not a good idea.

"It's fine," Veronica said. "I don't mind."

"See?" Dad said, reaching a hand into his pocket. "I'll even pay you for it if money's the issue."

"It's not for sale," Mom said, taking the bag and heading for the kitchen. As she passed me, she handed me her car keys. "Bring in the groceries. Then you can have your sandwich."

I didn't like her treating me like a little kid, but since Veronica was only a few feet away, "Thanks, Mom" was all I said.

Mom continued into the kitchen, and I headed for the door. Dad started after Mom to continue his battle for the sandwich. I had to stop him.

"Come on, Dad. You can help me with groceries," I said, then added a jab: "Unless that will aggravate your hernia too much."

Dad glared at me. I'd put him on the spot in front of Veronica, and he knew it. He could look old, weak, and injured, or he could flex what little muscles he had and carry in a couple bags of groceries. Somehow he summoned the strength to help me carry my groceries inside.

9

As Dad and I deposited the grocery bags on the center island of the kitchen, Mom unpacked them and put the food away in the refrigerator or the pantry. She'd bought enough food to feed a starving village in Africa for a month, if not more.

"Think you got enough?" I asked after carrying in the last two bags.

"Well, I don't want you to go hungry while you're here."

"I can't say that'll even be a remote possibility now."

Emptying a bag, I came across a plastic package containing a Gillette triple-bladed razor. I hadn't packed my razor and would probably need to shave by tomorrow at the latest.

"Oh, thanks for picking this up for me." I said to me.

"Oh, I didn't," Mom said. "I was hoping Veronica could shave Billy. I've never liked facial hair. But I can get one for you the next time I go to the store."

"Thanks," I said.

"What do you think you're doing?" Mom asked, but

she wasn't talking to me.

Dad had grabbed a green apple out of one of the bags he'd carried in. "I'm having an apple," he said.

Mom snatched it out of his hand. "The food is for Danny, not for you."

"But I'm hungry, and you won't let me have a sandwich."

"Then you should have packed a lunch."

"Why would I pack a lunch if there's food here?"

"It's not here for you. It's for Danny."

Dad turned to me. "You don't mind me grabbing an apple, do you, Danny Boy?"

I wasn't going to let either of them put me in the middle of this. I took the apple from Mom and handed it back to Dad.

Mom wasn't happy with that. "Danny—"

"It's a piece of fruit, Mom. I really don't care."

Dad smiled, polished the apple on his shirt, and said to me, "Thank you."

"You better wash that before you eat it," Mom told him.

Dad replied by taking a huge bite out of it as he left the kitchen. Mom was ready to go after him.

"Just let it go, Mom," I said. "It's not a big deal."

"You're right. And if he drops dead from any pesticides on it, it's his own fault."

Mom went back to putting the groceries away. I turned my attention to the bag filled with Sixth Street Deli deliciousness. Unwrapping the sandwich, I was greeted with the familiar French roll and the same smell I'd loved for years. As I prepared to take my first bite, Mom said, "Matt Henniker told me to say hello to you."

"Matt Henniker?" I hadn't seen Matt since we'd graduated high school.

Matt and I hadn't exactly been friends, but in a small town like Norco, everyone knew each other. Our senior year, we'd come to know each other a bit better. Both he and I, as well as countless other Norco boys, had been tantalized, manipulated, and deceived by the beautiful and deceptive April Lanning. April had shown me clearly how deceitful the female of our species can be. Unfortunately, I'd later forgotten that hard-learned lesson.

Matt had been a hell of a pitcher in high school. We'd played Little League together years before that. We were on the Minor B Astros. Even then, it was obvious to everyone that Matt had skills on the field unlike anyone else. By the time we made it to high school, there was little doubt in anyone's minds that Matt would likely go pro.

After graduation, I'd run into him at the old Ranchland grocery store, where he'd worked as a box boy. He'd told me was that he'd be going to Cal State Fullerton on a baseball scholarship. That had to be 1998, which seemed like a lifetime ago.

"Was he shopping or working at Stater's?" I asked Mom.

"He's the general manager of the new store down the

street."

I guessed baseball hadn't panned out for Matt after all. I probably should've felt bad for him. I didn't. Having an overabundance of talent doesn't guarantee that you'll make it big. I knew that all too well. But at least I was still playing and doing what I loved and not working in a grocery store like he'd been doing since he was seventeen.

"Good to see he's been able to move up the food chain," I said.

My comment must've offended Mom. "He's become a very respected member of the community," she said.

"I didn't mean it like it came out." Uh… I actually did, so I added, "Matt's a good guy."

"Yes, he is. And he said if there's anything he can help with, just let him know."

"Yeah. Sounds good," I said with zero intention of connecting with Matt for the ten days I'd be in Norco. For that matter, there wasn't anyone in or around town I wanted to see socially. I wasn't one to reminisce on the past, even about one or two of the better lays I'd had. I didn't want to relive it or reconnect with anyone from the old days. I didn't see the point to any of that.

But when did I ever really get what I wanted?

10

PROJECT NURSE STAYED UNTIL FIVE thirty.

During her first day on the job, I learned how to inject ground-up food into Billy's gut, but passed on giving the Prick a sponge bath. Veronica could do that... and if she was lucky, she might be able to do something similar yet more sensual to me.

I also saw firsthand that I didn't have to worry about Dad pulling a Rusty and bogarting Project Nurse from me. Dad had no game whatsoever. While I still didn't want to think about it, he never would have scored with Mom if she hadn't been a serious drinker when they met.

When it came time for Veronica to leave, Mom hugged her and thanked her for everything. Dad came over to her, took Veronica's hand in his, and kissed it.

"Okay, James," Veronica said. "I'll see you tomorrow."

"I can hardly wait," Dad said, and kissed her hand one more time.

"You should probably apply some sanitizer before you go," Mom told Veronica.

Dad threw Mom a look, and Veronica smiled slightly at

me.

"Let me help you out," I said, grabbing her cooler.

"Okay," she said as she flung the strap of her bag over her shoulder.

Once we were out front, I said to her, "Feel free to give my dad the smackdown whenever you want."

"Oh, he's cute."

"He's a lot of things. Cute I'm not so sure about."

She opened the driver's-side door of a 4Runner parked in front of the house. "You've got my number," she said. "If anything happens with Billy or you have any questions, just give me a call or a text."

"I'll be sure to do that."

"You know, other than the catheter incident, you did pretty good today."

"Thanks for reminding me about that."

"Don't worry," she said with a slightly mischievous grin. "I'm sure you'll get it right tomorrow."

"I can hardly wait."

"Oh, and you should talk to him."

"I'm about talked out with my dad."

"Not him. Billy."

Uh…

I couldn't say that would be happening, so I deflected.

"He doesn't seem too talkative right now."

"I know, but like I told your mom, a lot of patients say they remember people talking to them. For all we know, it helps them keep up the will to fight and to live."

"All right," I said. "I'll be sure to have a nice chat with him later."

I wasn't sure how nice it would be. I didn't have anything nice I'd like to say to the Prick. Though if it could help him come to and recover, it might be worth a shot. But I didn't want him to come to too fast right. I still had this incredible project to work to completion.

Veronica climbed into the driver's seat and started up the 4Runner.

"See you tomorrow, Danny Boy," she said, and closed the door.

Arrr! I hated the nickname, and now she was calling me it!

I wanted to tell her never to call me that again but resisted. I thought I stood on solid ground with her. Yet I wasn't entirely sure.

Before she drove off, Veronica looked over at me and waved. That was a good sign. It verified I'd been playing things the right way. I gave a small wave back, and she headed off down the street.

I walked back to the house, but when I reached the front door, I heard a car come to a stop behind me. Maybe Veronica had forgotten something. I turned not to see Project Nurse returning to offer me her body, but to find a silver Honda Accord parking by the mailbox.

The man behind the Honda's wheel smiled and nodded his chin up at me.

I wasn't sure who it was at first and didn't wave back.

A moment later, I recognized him.

Sergio Luna.

Sergio Luna, the drummer who had been with me when I started my first band. Sergio Luna, my once best friend that I had not seen or talked to in years.

Of all the people I didn't want to run into while in Norco, Sergio sat near the top of the list.

What in the hell was he doing there?

11

"THE ONE AND ONLY DANNY MACK," Sergio said as he climbed out of the Honda. He had a big smile on his face and appeared genuinely happy to see me.

"Serg?" I said. He'd put on at least thirty pounds since I'd last seen him, making his belly bulge. His dark hair was still thick, but flecked with a grey on the sides.

"It's good to see you, man," Sergio said.

"Yeah, you too," I said, trying to convince myself of this.

I offered him my hand to shake. Sergio pushed past it and threw his arms around me in a big hug. Any animosity I thought Sergio might have toward me wasn't there.

"What brings you by?" I asked after our surprise embrace.

"Tina called me up. She asked if I'd come by and pray for Billy tonight."

The first part made sense. I could see my sister pushing Sergio my way. She enjoyed picking other people's scabs and seeing how much they'd bleed. The second part of Sergio's statement baffled me.

"You do that often?" I asked.

"Quite a bit, actually," he said, his smile enlarging. "I guess you hadn't heard. I'm a pastor now."

"Shut the fuu—" I stopped myself before I dropped the full-on F-Bomber. "Sorry... That was just a bit surprising to hear."

Sergio took it in stride. "I was just as surprised as anybody when I wound up getting ordained. But as the Bible says, a man makes plans in his heart, but the Lord directs his steps."

"Yeah, I guess so."

"My dad and mom were pretty happy. Especially when he decided to hand his church off to me."

"I bet," I said, looking away and hoping to avoid any religious talk deeper than this.

Sergio must've picked up on this, as he kindly steered the conversation elsewhere. "The circumstances suck, but it really is good to see you."

"Yeah. It's been a while," I said.

"How long's it been? Ten years?"

"Almost twelve." I looked down at the concrete of the driveway. This wasn't a place I wanted to go either.

"No. It can't be that long."

"Will be twelve in August."

"Wow. I guess time does fly."

"Yeah."

But this conversation wasn't. I didn't want to discuss the past. I didn't want to catch up on what I'd been doing.

I didn't want to get into any of that crap.

And for the first time in years, someone in my family finally had good timing and saved me. Tina's Audi pulled into the driveway and effectively ended that discussion with Sergio.

"How'd the first day go?" Tina asked as she got out of the car and made her way over to us.

"Just like old times," I said. "You annoyed the hell out of me, Mom and Dad argued over nothing of importance, and Billy pissed all over me."

"That's not very funny," she said with a scowl.

"The truth seldom is."

Tina hugged Sergio. "Thanks for coming by. I hope I'm not late."

"You're fine," he said. "I just got here and was catching up with Danny."

"Good. I'm sure you two have plenty to talk about."

Guess she'd noticed my scab hadn't come off enough to bleed. I wasn't in the mood for Tina's crap and decided to push her buttons for a change.

"Yeah," I said to Sergio. "You should see the nurse Tina hired to help me take care of Billy. She's easily a nine in her scrubs, and I'm guessing a ten-plus in anything or nothing else."

"You're unbelievable," Tina said. "You are aware he's a pastor now, right?

I looked at Sergio. "Does that come with a vow of celibacy?"

"That's a Catholic priest," Sergio said. "I'm a non-denominational pastor."

"See?" I said to Tina. "No harm, no foul."

"That said," Sergio added, "looking at a woman to lust after her isn't on the list of approved activities. Especially when you're married."

Sergio held up his left hand, wiggling his ring finger, where a thick gold wedding band was.

Dammit.

My desire to taunt Tina had backfired. I'd accidentally walked headfirst into another topic I wanted to avoid. My only choice was to say something they both might find slightly offensive.

"Then you probably don't want me to give you too much detail about her ass."

"You're such a pig," Tina said, full of disgust.

"All those 4H kids always told us that pigs were smarter than dogs," I said.

"Yet they still sleep in their own feces," Tina fired back.

That was a good one. I didn't have a fast comeback.

Tina allowed herself a smirk. She knew she'd won that exchange. She turned to Sergio. "Are you ready?"

"Whenever you are," he said.

"How long do you think that'll take?" I asked.

"I'm not sure," he said. "Prayer really doesn't come with minimum or maximum time limits."

"Okay, well, while you're doing that, I'm going to run

down to Target and pick up some clothes."

Tina said, "You can go to Target when we're done praying."

"I feel like going now."

"But Sergio came over so we can pray for Billy."

"I get that, but I'm not much of a prayer."

"Our baby brother is fighting for his life. He needs as much prayer as he can get."

"Then throw a few in for me while I'm at the store."

Tina was about to go off on me, but Sergio prevented that from happening.

"Danny probably needs to get out and take a little break," he said.

Tina looked at me. She was weighing whether to agree with Sergio or lash out and rip my face off.

I played for her sympathy, hoping she had some. "I really do need to get out of here for a while," I said.

"Okay," she said. "But don't be gone too long. I can't stay late."

"I'll be there and back before you know it. I'll even take Billy's Supra. I'm sure that can haul some ass."

"What's wrong with your car?" Tina asked.

"Nothing. But if I'm in charge of everything, then I'm taking Billy's car."

12

YES, BILLY'S TOYOTA SUPRA HAD some serious *huevos*.

And that's from someone who's far from a car guy.

Tina didn't want me to take his Supra. I didn't care or need her permission.

Billy had taken my first car for a fateful spin without my permission back when. It was only fair that I even up the score now that the opportunity had presented itself. Plus, I'd stayed to take care of his dumb ass. Using his car was a small bit of compensation. He could never fully pay me back for all the things he'd taken from me.

Seeing Sergio had brought back a flood of feelings and their associated memories. It took all of my strength to force them deep down where they belonged. He'd been my best friend for years. We'd met in the third grade when his family moved to Norco from San Antonio to start a church. He started learning to play the drums in junior high about the same time I got serious about the guitar.

By the time we'd moved up the street to the high school, we'd put together a quartet. Our friend Tim played bass, and our buddy Geoff the keyboards. We called ourselves The Regulators, since we were all fans of the two *Young Guns* movies. It was a fun learning experience. But as one drunken jock who was also a very vocal music critic yelled during the first party we played, "You guys suck shit through a straw!"

While that criticism wasn't constructive, it wasn't necessarily inaccurate.

I put more time into practice and proceeded to go through a variety of bass players and keyboardists. Finally, we found Lonnie. He was damn good on the bass. The three of us jelled exceptionally well. But we ran through a variety of keyboardists and never could find the right person for the position.

It was a good run for quite a while. We were good enough to get gigs at various clubs and got to play at the Norco Fair and during Horseweek. It wasn't a lot of money, but it was enough that none of us had to get stupid jobs like the rest of our friends who hadn't gone off to college. I'd written a dozen songs that we wanted to record. A couple of them were even requested when we played at clubs. I could feel it. We were on the brink of something big. Really big.

Then the band's road trip happened. Or maybe it's more accurate to say I came back from that tour and found out that Billy had stuck it in me good. As much as I wanted to, I'd never forget that Saturday morning. I packed up everything important to me and headed to Nashville the next day, effectively breaking up the band

and ruining my friendships with all my bandmates. I didn't care. I didn't want any contact with anyone from Norco after what had happened. And with few exceptions, I'd managed to keep it that way.

Dammit.

How had I let my mind drag me through all of those stupid memories?

I grabbed my phone and brought up Big Paul's number. I hadn't heard from him and was curious how things had gone the previous night. My call went to voice mail. It was after six. He should've been up. I left him a message to get back to me as I pulled into the Target shopping center. Some of the shops were different than the ones I remembered, but Denny's and the Staples were still there.

Inside Target, I picked up a little red basket and went over to the *Sexual Health* aisle. In previous years that section had been called *Family Planning*. I'd always thought *Family Prevention* was a better title, but it seemed that *Sexual Health* was now the acceptable term.

I grabbed a box of a dozen Trojans for use with Project Nurse in the not-too-distant future then headed for the rear of the store, where the men's clothing section had always been. That's when I heard someone say, "Danny Meacham? Hot damn, is that really you?"

I turned to find a chubby guy with long hair pushing a shopping cart. He seemed to be about my age, so I probably should've known him. I didn't have a clue who he might be.

"Oh, hey," I said anyway. People often approached me knowing who I was, but I didn't know them. It comes with living your life on stage and connecting with an audience of strangers.

Chubby came over and gave me an immense bear hug that cracked my back. "Damn, it's good to see you," he said.

"Yeah, you too." *Whoever you are.*

"I'm really sorry to hear what happened to your brother. You got any news on him?"

"Probably nothing more than what you've heard."

"You know there's a big group of us on Facebook, and we're all praying for him. Hey. How come you and I aren't friends on Facebook?"

"Well, I'd have to be on it for that to happen."

"Oh, I'm on Twitter and Instagram too."

"I'm not really into the social media thing."

"What? A big-time singer like you? How can you not be on social media?"

Now I was really confused about who this was but didn't want to show it.

"One of the guys in my band handles it for us," I explained.

"Gotcha. So I guess you came to town to see Billy."

"Yeah. I'm kind of taking care of him."

"Oh man, that's so awesome of you."

"It's something," I said, finally reaching the point

where I couldn't pretend to know who this was any longer. "Uh, don't take this the wrong way, but I'm having a hard time placing your name."

Chubby looked hurt. "Dude, you don't remember me?"

"I didn't say that. It's just not coming to me all that fast."

"Omar, man. Omar Vargas."

"Oh…Omar." I remembered Omar. He was an annoying loudmouth jackass who was extremely desperate for attention all through high school. Behind his back, everyone called him "Circ-Ass Varg-Ass." It was an extremely on-the-nose parody of Circus Vargas, which rolled through the area every year or so, but it fit.

"Yeah, I know I've gotten a lot bigger since we graduated."

"Oh, I can't say that's true," I said, not knowing why I was trying to humor the now Fat-Ass Circ-Ass Varg-Ass.

"I hit the gym quite a bit," he said.

And probably the McDonald's drive-thru on the way there and back.

Omar pulled out his phone. "Can I get a selfie with you?"

"Actually… I just stopped in to pick up some stuff, and I've got to get back to Billy."

My words made him take a look into the basket I held. He saw my Trojans and smiled broadly. "Check you out, stud. Looks like you're going to be taking care of a little more than Billy."

I didn't feel like having this conversation any longer. "Have a good one, Omar. I gotta go."

I turned my back on him and headed down the aisle the opposite way I'd been going simply to get away from him. I hadn't wanted to run into anyone from Norco, but now Sergio had shown up, and Omar had found me in the *Sexual Health* aisle. Hopefully, that would be the last encounter with anyone from the old days.

But as we all know, bad things happen in threes.

13

Little delays have an interesting impact on life.

You can't find your car keys and are running five minutes later than you should be, but that meant you avoided a major accident you might have mangled you.

You're waiting for a ride at the movie theater because your dad forgot to pick you up, and by being stuck there, you meet your first girlfriend up in the arcade.

Or you run into Circ-Ass Varg-Ass at Target, and that puts you in exactly the wrong place at the wrong time.

Back in the men's clothing section, I threw a jumbo pack of boxer briefs into my basket on top of the Trojans. Next, I found a couple pairs of Wranglers. In the country scene, anything other than Wrangler is taboo. I'm not sure how that came about, as I'd never had a problem with Levi's, but I had to keep my country image intact, even if I wasn't on stage.

Target also had a good selection of pop culture T-shirts. Many had superheroes or *Star Wars* characters on them. Others were throwbacks to things from the 60s, 70s, 80s, and 90s. They also had shirts of a musical sort. I put three into my basket—one of Johnny Cash, another of Sun Records, and the last of Guns N' Roses. GNR may not be country, but it didn't matter. They were GNR and I'd spent hours upon hours learning how to play "Sweet Child o' Mine" in my teens.

Now, having found what I'd come for, I should have gone directly to the checkout. But no. I made the mistake of stopping to browse through the music section.

While times had changed and most people got their music by download, stores like Target still sold CDs. Their selection typically wasn't that good. They carried only very mainstream music with nothing all that original, usually compilations and greatest hits bullshit, but that didn't matter. Music was an essential part of my life. I'd always look. You never know when you'd find a gem.

I missed the music stores. I could spend hours in the Wherehouse, Music Plus, and the Mad Platter as a teenager. The world didn't know what it had lost when music had gone digital. It wasn't just that the sound quality was as degraded as the artists' royalties. It was the experience of searching out music, holding an album or CD in your hands, and exploring it in its entirety. Something was missing by simply sampling a song or getting computer-generated recommendations for what you might also like. If that had been the case, I never would have discovered Lyle Lovett or Shooter Jennings.

Seeing nothing worth purchasing, I stepped out of the music section and started for the checkout aisles.

That was when I ran into the Slut.

She stood in the middle of the main aisle pushing a red cart. A blonde girl maybe about five sat in the reverse seat by the handle. Mom had told me that she'd had another kid with the guy she married.

Her shopping cart came to a halt as soon as she saw me. I stood there frozen too. The surprise of seeing me was evident on her face I'm sure it was on mine too. I'd never expected to run into her there. If I had, I wouldn't have left Billy's house at all.

I don't know why, but Jessie still mesmerized me. She wore her natural blonde hair shorter than before. She'd gained a little weight, but she wasn't fat. Oddly enough, it made her face and body fuller in a good way. Crows-feet though had found their way to the corners of her captivating blue eyes. Worry lines also creased her forehead. Maybe life wasn't all that perfect or as cheery for her.

Good. The Slut didn't deserve to be happy.

"Hi, Danny," she said hesitantly.

I didn't reply. It wasn't that I didn't have plenty to say. Oh, I sure as hell did. Something inside me mysteriously restrained my tongue.

My silence and stony stare must've added to her discomfort, so she spoke again.

"I heard you'd come back."

Yeah, I'm sure she had.

I still didn't say anything.

"Anything new with Billy?" she asked.

The sound of the Prick's name coming across her deceitful lips sent me over the edge. After all these years, the time had come for me to let her have it. But before I could, a young boy popped out of a nearby aisle with some video game in his hand.

It was the Kid.

I'd never seen him in person before. I wish it had remained that way.

"Mom, can I get this?" he asked Jessie.

She turned to answer him and I changed my strategy. Rather than unleashing on the Slut, I decided this was the perfect time to exit stage right. I spun away from them, put my head down, and marched as fast as I could to the front of the store and the exit doors.

Why the hell was I so stupid to stop and look at the music I knew would be shit? Why didn't I just log on to Amazon and order some clothes online?

Why was Jessie shopping here when she doesn't even live in Norco anymore?

Why? Why? WHY?????

14

I GOT BACK TO THE Prick's house and was relieved to find Sergio's Accord gone. Unfortunately, Mom's, Dad's, and Tina's cars were all still there. I hoped not to have any interactions with any of them, but that wasn't the way the evening was going.

Tina had set up a makeshift office in the living room beside Billy's bed. Papers and file folders were spread out on the carpet at her feet. She sat in the big, comfy chair with her computer in her lap.

She looked up at me. "I thought you went to buy some clothes?"

Damn. My hands were empty. In my hurry to get away from the Slut and the Kid, I'd ditched my basket in housewares before rushing out of the store.

I shrugged, attempting to play it off. "Didn't see anything I really liked. I'll order something online."

Tina's eyes narrowed. She knew I was lying. That ability probably came in good in her profession.

I didn't want an inquisition. I turned away from her and headed for the stairs.

Ahead of me in the family room, Dad looked at me from the sofa. "Danny Boy, what do you think about ordering up some Chinese?"

I answered him as I went up the stairs, "Whatever you want. I'm not hungry."

I went into the master bedroom and shut the door firmly, being careful not to slam it. I just needed to be away from everyone. I had to clear my head and block out any memories of the interaction at Target before they could solidify.

Stupidly, I'd picked the wrong room to do that. I'd forgotten about the pictures of the Prick with the Slut and the Kid that hung on the wall. The three of them all looked so happy. They all looked so loving. They all looked like more bullshit than I cared to deal with. They all looked like they needed to come down immediately.

I took a step toward the wall, and my phone rang. I wanted to ignore it, but maybe it was Big Paul finally getting back to me. Or maybe it was the hospital saying that they'd reviewed Billy's vital stats and there was no chance on him waking up and that I should just pull the plug.

Nope. None of the above. The caller ID read *Mom*.

Mom?

Why was she calling me when she was only downstairs?

"Yeah, Mom," I said, hoping to hide the anger and stress in my voice when I answered.

"Danny, what's wrong?"

"Nothing. I just needed to use the bathroom really bad and didn't want to stink up the bottom floor."

"You're not on the pot right now, are you?"

"Of course not."

"Good, because it would be rude to answer while doing your business."

"I'm not one of those people. You raised me better than that."

"Yes, I did. Now, will you be coming down anytime soon?"

"Actually… I think I just want to be alone for the rest of the night."

There was a pause, then she said. "Do you want to talk about what happened at Target?"

"What do you mean what happened at Target?"

"Jessie called and said you ran into her and Mason, and that didn't go all that well."

What in the hell?

I disconnected the call, went out the door, and stood on the landing, looking down at where Mom stood still on her cell phone. Tina looked up at me from the comfy chair where she worked.

"Oh, she just happened to call you and tell you that?" I asked, the rage building in me.

"She was worried about you," Mom said.

"Like she gives a damn about me. And she shouldn't be calling you in the first place."

Mom gave me a stern look. "Regardless of how you

feel about Jessie, she is still the mother of my grandson."

Argh.

"Fine," I said. "You want to talk to her or whatever, that's up to you, but I don't ever want to hear about it."

I turned around, went back into the bedroom, and this time quite purposefully slammed the damn door.

Yeah, dramatic, I know. But I was pissed.

I crossed the room and, one by one, took all the pictures down. I considered setting them on the floor and turning them around to face the wall. That way they would no longer silently taunt me. But they'd still be there. I'd still see them, even through the backs of the frames.

I opened the lower drawer of the dresser. An odd assortment of poorly folded clothes half filled it. I tossed the clothes on the floor and started putting the pictures into the drawer.

There was a knock at the door. Then I heard Tina say, "Danny, can I come in?"

"No."

My sister ignored my answer and entered anyway. "Danny—"

"Tina. Don't."

"Look, I know how you feel about her. What she and Billy did was wrong—"

"You're damn right. And if you hadn't invited her to your little party—"

"I'm sorry you ran into them, but don't try and—"

"You're sorry?" I yelled. "What the hell was she even

doing there when she doesn't even live in town anymore?"

"Actually, she does," Tina said. "She and the kids moved in with her mom a few months ago."

"And you just happened to forget to mention that important little detail to me?"

"You forbid all of us from talking to you about her, so why would you want me to tell you about her divorce?"

Tina was right. The Slut was a forbidden topic of discussion with me. So naturally she used that to keep her return to Norco from me. It was best to let that drop, but of course I had to take a dig.

"So," I said, "She ruined another relationship, huh? There's another non-surprise."

"That's not what happened. It was him and it was quite the scandal actually."

"I don't care to know the details."

"You don't need to, but your acting like this isn't helping Mom's stress levels."

"Mom's stress levels? What about my stress levels?"

"Danny, all I'm trying to do is help."

"You wanna help me out, big sis?"

"Of course."

"Good. Then help me by leaving for the night. And take the parents with you."

Tina looked at her watch. "It's not even eight o'clock."

"I know, but I haven't slept in almost two days. And if I don't get some sleep, I'm gonna lose my mind."

"Okay, but—"

"No, buts. Please, Tina. I just need to be alone and get some sleep." I could see she was still going to resist, so I laid it on the best I could. "If you want to help, big sis, then help me make that happen. Please."

She looked at me for a long moment and surprised me by softly answering, "Okay."

15

DESPITE THEIR RELUCTANCE TO VACATE the premises, Tina got Mom to go home and Dad to the house where he rented a room. Once I was convinced that none of them would be coming back inside because they'd "accidentally" forgotten something, I went downstairs.

The house was quiet except for the machines connected to Billy. I stood at the foot of the bed and stared down at the Prick. Veronica had said I should talk to him and let it come naturally. Fine. I'd try it.

"You know I still hate you," I said.

My words were honest. As honest as they'd been when I last saw Billy face to face after everything here fell apart.

A few months after I'd relocated to Nashville, Mom had her heart attack.

Tina's call had woken me up in the middle of the night. Much like the one Mom had made to me about Billy two days ago, Tina was in tears and wasn't sure if Mom was going to make it. There might not be enough time for me to drive cross-country and see Mom while she was still alive. I managed to get an overpriced United flight to LAX for the next day.

Mom was in surgery at the hospital in Riverside when my plane landed. Dad drove out in his Oldsmobile and picked me up. Naturally, he didn't have money for gas. I had to whip out the MasterCard again to fill up the tank to get us out to Norco.

That was a hard trip. Not so much because of Mom's condition, which improved remarkably after her surgery and my arrival. The problem, as always, was Billy. I refused to have any contact with the Prick.

Tina had promised that if I came home, she'd keep us away from each other. Billy still lived at home, so with what little credit was left on my MasterCard, I booked a room at the Howard Johnson's on the other side of town. True to her word, Tina arranged things so that Billy and I would not be visiting the hospital at the same time.

That worked out for about a week. Once Mom was on the mend, the hospital discharged her. There was no way I could go to the house and see her without running into the Prick. Tina said she'd arrange it so Billy would leave so I could come over and see Mom. I was constantly on guard, fearing he'd break that agreement he'd made with our sister. Three days into Mom's return home, he did.

When I arrived at the house that Wednesday morning, Billy stepped out the front door.

"Hey, bro," the Prick said to me. "We should talk."

I let my fist do the talking and took a swing at him.

Unfortunately for me, I hadn't been in many fights and

missed completely.

Billy, however, had been in more than he could probably count. He hammered me pretty good. Mr. Cargill, who had been cutting his lawn across the street, ran over and broke up our melee. He pulled Billy off me and held him back, waiting for him to calm down.

Catching his breath, Billy looked up at me and said, "Hey... I'm sorry."

"And I hate you," I said, not at all surprised by the words that had come out of me. It was the punch I threw that came out of nowhere.

This time my fist connected with the Prick's nose and produced a fair amount of blood.

I saw the rage in his eyes. He broke free of Mr. Cargill and rushed me but stopped when Jessie yelled, "Billy! Stop!"

Jessie's voice caused us both to turn. She stood in the doorway of the house, very large, very pregnant, and very frightened.

"I'm sorry, babe," Billy told her.

I used that moment to take off down the street and spent the rest of the day walking back to the Howard Johnson's. Tina was waiting for me when I got there. She assured me that Billy and the Slut had left and that Mom wanted to see me. I agreed to go back to the house, but only because I wanted Mom to hear it straight from me that I was going back to Nashville in the morning.

I spent an hour with Mom and broke that news to her.

She didn't want me to go but understood. Tina gave me a ride back to the motel to gather my stuff and check out, then drove me out to LAX. She wanted to talk, but I refused to listen, turning the radio up as loud as I could until she got the point that there was nothing to discuss.

She dropped me off at the United terminal. It would be over a year until I saw Tina or Mom or Dad. I didn't have any reasons to come home again. I didn't want to risk running into Billy or Jessie or their kid. I didn't come home for Sergio's wedding, Mom's sixtieth birthday party, or my ten-year high school reunion.

I was done with Norco.

Except for Mom, I didn't want to see any people from there ever again. I didn't care if I didn't see Tina or Dad either, though they'd proven impossible to avoid. Everyone who had been part of my life in Norco needed to be left in the past.

But the past wasn't done having its fun and games with me that night.

16

AFTER BEING UP NEARLY TWO days straight, I could feel myself dozing off once my head landed on the pillow.

That was when the voices started.

Initially, I thought they were dream voices, but it turned out they weren't coming from inside my head. They came from outside. Outside the house. From real people.

I got out of bed and separated the Venetian blinds to look down into the backyard, just as a goateed naked man cannonballed into the swimming pool. He joined a bald tattooed dude. There was also a woman a few years younger than them in the pool. None of them had any clothing on.

Why are there naked people swimming in the pool? Am I hallucinating?

The sight of the lone woman's ample breasts popping above the waterline made it clear I wasn't. There were three people skinny-dipping out back in the Prick's pool.

Without throwing on pants or a shirt, I hurried downstairs and outside to confront them. The uninvited sausage party didn't even notice me standing there in my BVDs until I yelled, "What the hell are you doing here?"

They all stopped and turned to look at me.

"Who the hell are you?" Baldie asked me.

"I'm the guy who's asking you what the hell you're doing here."

"No, dude," Baldie said, "what are *you* doing here?"

This guy was dense.

"Did you seriously just ask me that?" I replied.

"Yeah, 'cause I know this ain't your house."

"You're right. And it isn't yours either, so what are you doing here?"

"I asked you first, dude."

There was no use talking to this moron.

"I'm calling the cops," I said, and turned back to the house.

"Good, 'cause this is my buddy Billy's house, and your ass is trespassing."

I spun back around to them. "Oh, so you're Billy's friends?"

"We're pretty much like his best friends."

"And I'm definitely *like* his brother."

The goateed guy who'd remained silent throughout my exchange with Baldie spoke up. "Danny? That you?"

Great, another person I didn't recognize who knew me. "Yeah. And who the hell are you?"

"It's me, man. Eric Parker," he said with a broad grin.

Oh yes, of course, Eric Parker. The second biggest

stoner loser of Norco High, right behind my brother. Billy and Eric were partners in crime. And that wasn't some cute moniker. They were petty criminals throughout their unproductive high school careers. If I'd had my way, they both would have been sent to juvie for the crap they pulled.

Eric had been quite lean when we were growing up, but his face was rounder now, as he'd put on a few pounds in the years since I'd seen him.

"It's been a long time," Eric said.

I wanted to say not long enough but instead went back to my original question: "What the hell are you all doing here?"

"Not much going on tonight, so we figured we'd swing by for a dip," Eric said.

"No, I mean, why are you doing that here in Billy's pool?"

"Billy's cool with it, man," Eric said. "He always says his casa is mi casa."

"Oh, and have you talked to Billy lately?"

Eric thought about it then said, "A couple weeks ago."

"Not since?" I asked.

"Nope. He's been radio silent."

"And do you have any idea why that might be?"

Eric shrugged. "That's Billy. Sometimes he just takes off for a few weeks, doesn't say where he's going or where he's been, then he shows up with some bitchin' stories."

"And do you have any clue where Billy might be right

now?

"Maui?" Baldie said. No wonder he and Billy got along. They had an equal amount of brain cells.

"For your information," I said, "he's inside."

"He's here?" the woman asked.

Dealing with Dipshit One and Dipshit Two, I'd completely ignored the naked woman standing in the water.

"That's right," I said to her. I really must've been tired, especially since she had quite the nice rack floating in the water. She was maybe thirty and definitely cute, despite the fact that both her arms were covered with tats.

Baldie broke me away from my thoughts when he said, "Then tell Billy to get his ass out here."

"Oh, I'm sure he would," I said, "but he's hooked up to a machine that's keeping him breathing."

They all looked genuinely stunned.

"Aren't any of you on Facebook?" I asked, sounding like Circ-Ass Varg-Ass.

"No way," Baldie said. "That's just a way for the government to keep tabs on you."

That was probably the most intelligent thing that idiot had ever said, but I couldn't give him that credit. "Well, if you were on Facebook, then you'd know that Billy hit a telephone pole two Saturdays ago. He's been in a coma ever since."

"Bullshit," Eric said.

"Put your clothes on and come and see for yourself."

17

"YO, BILL," ERIC SAID AS the three trespassers hovered around Billy's hospital bed.

I'd found towels, and once the three had dried off and dressed, I'd brought them into the living room to see the Prick. The buxom, tattooed woman stepped closer to Billy's bed. "Can he hear us?" she asked me.

"I really don't know."

I saw the tears well up in her eyes.

Hmm. Interesting.

"Are you and him… an item or whatever?" I asked.

I'd never gotten into chicks with a lot of tattoos, even though that had become quite common in recent years, but she was cute and could probably be a fun little side project. Maybe.

"Sometimes," she said. "Just not exclusive."

That answer instantly disqualified her from the potential project list. She might've been somewhat cute and bouncing a nice pair of twins, but another of my rules was never to go where Billy had gone before.

"Man, this really sucks," Baldie said.

"That's a pretty succinct way of putting it," I said.

"Thanks," he said, not realizing I had insulted him.

"What's the chance he's gonna wake up?" Eric asked.

"No one knows."

"This really does suck," Eric said.

We all stood around Billy quietly for a long time. Then Baldie pulled a lighter and a pipe out of his pocket. Before he could put the lighter to his weed, I said, "Whoa. What the hell are you doing?"

"It's cool. It's legal now. Plus, I've got a medical card."

"No," I said. "It's not cool and I don't care what the law is."

"Yeah, Tommy," Billy's Sometimes-Girl said. "We can smoke out back."

"No," I said. "I don't want you smoking here at all. As a matter of fact, I want all of you gone."

"Billy doesn't mind if we're here," Eric said.

"Well, he left me in charge, and I do, so you all need to get out of here. And if I catch you in the backyard again, I will be calling the cops."

"Oh come on, dude," Bald Tommy said. "We're Billy's friends."

"That's a horrible argument to make with me," I said. "You've got two minutes to grab your stuff and get the hell out of here or I'm calling 911 about three intruders in the backyard. I might even accidentally say they look black."

That threat worked. The trio headed toward the back

door. As they were about to step out, Eric turned back to me and asked, "You mind if we come by and see him, you know, like, during the day?"

"Yeah. I mind a lot."

Eric clearly didn't like my answer, but he followed Bald Tommy outside. Billy's Sometimes-Girl stopped at the sliding glass door and faced me. She stood there, staring at me. It made me feel uncomfortable.

"What?" I asked her.

"You and Billy look a lot alike," she said.

"Unfortunately so."

"But you're nothing like him."

"Well, that I'll take as a compliment."

"It wasn't. He's a cool guy. You're a complete asshole."

18

I'M A COMPLETE ASSHOLE? I'm *a complete asshole?*

Who was that tatted-up ho to judge me? Did she have a clue who Billy really was? Did she know any of the crap he'd pulled in his life?

Of course not. She was a stoner skank. Her opinion didn't mean jack.

Yet her parting words got my adrenaline pumping in overdrive. I had too much energy and couldn't go back to bed. I knew I wouldn't be able to sleep till I calmed down. I stayed downstairs and hoped something on TV could bore me into a slumber.

I plopped down on the sofa, grabbed the remote, and clicked on the ginormous TV. I sped through the channels, looking for something to zone out on, and someone caught my eye on CNN. I flipped back a couple of channels to it.

The guest being interviewed stood out in front of Los Angeles City Hall. I didn't know L.A. well, but I knew the building from *Dragnet* reruns I'd watched with Mom as a kid. I also recognized the interviewee without having to read the name below him. Corey Foster.

Corey was also a Norco High Class of '98 graduate and another one of April's Fools. Corey's dad had been on the Norco City Council for years—still might have been for all I knew—so no one was really surprised when Corey had gone into politics himself. Still, I was a little surprised to see him on CNN right now. At least someone I knew from growing up had had their life turn out as they'd planned it.

Corey was arguing against Trump's new immigration policy, which he kept referring to as a "Muslim Ban." I went up a couple of channels to check on FOX News. Not because I agreed more with their political slant than CNN's. Politics had never interested me. I doubted it ever would. I'd tuned to FOX wondering if April Lanning would be on. It would be funny if she were on there while Corey appeared on the opposition channel. She wasn't. It was some weird panel show. I continued to channel-surf.

There wasn't anything I found worth watching. I pulled up Netflix, which confirmed Billy's tastes were far different from mine. It recommended *Friday After Next*, *Nacho Libre*, and some show called *Hot Rod Unlimited*. I didn't have the patience to look through anything else it might offer up. I chose to find something to watch the old-fashioned way.

I went to the shelf beside the TV and looked through Billy's extensive DVD collection. Most of his flicks were stupid 90's action flicks. Naturally, he had all the *Fast and Furious* movies. I'd enjoyed the first one but the second sucked, so I'd given up on those movies. Billy did have both the original and the prequel *Star Wars* trilogies, plus that new movie, *The Force Awakens*. I guessed we had that in common, but I wasn't sure I was in the mood for any galaxy far, far away action.

I continued to thumb through the Prick's DVDs until I came across one in clear plastic case without a label. Was it some weird custom-order porno or snuff film that people with ridiculous money and even more ridiculous sexual tastes purchased? I wasn't quite sure that would be Billy's style.

Oh no.

Had he made his own Kardashian-style sex tape?

I sincerely hoped not.

Given those speculations, I should have left the DVD sitting there between *The Transporter* and *Walk Hard*, but it had stoked my curiosity. I pulled it from its place between the other traditional DVD cases and could see a title written on the silver front of the disk. In black Sharpie marker and block letter printing, it read: *Mason & Me*.

I pushed the DVD back in its spot and continued my search for something watchable. Billy had all eight *Harry Potter* movies. Interesting. I didn't see the Prick as a Harry Potter fan. Not enough explosions or T&A. I, on the other hand, had seen them all multiple times. Granted, the books were much better, but the movies were still good, especially by the time they got to *Prisoner of Azkaban*.

I looked to the left and found all three *Toy Story* movies and *The Incredibles*.

Ah. These weren't Billy's movies. They belonged to the Kid.

For a moment I considered watching *The Incredibles*— I'd heard good things about it—but wasn't in the mood for a cartoon. I played it safe and popped the first *Star Wars* movie in the DVD player. That would calm me down. I'd seen it enough times that it would be easy for me to fall asleep while trying to watch it.

Wrong.

19

I'D WOUND UP WATCHING STAR WARS, Empire, and was up the point in *Jedi* where the Ewoks were seasoning Han Solo for their banquet when the first rays of morning light caught my eye. How was it possible that I hadn't fallen asleep?

I knew I'd be dragging more today than I had yesterday, but I still couldn't sleep, so I finished watching *Return of the Jedi*, wishing, as I always did, that George Lucas hadn't made so many unnecessary changes to the end of the movie. If he was going to replace old Anakin with young Anakin, why not do the same with Obi-Wan and Yoda?

Mom called and said she was on the way over and asked if I needed anything. I told her a quad-shot caramel macchiato from Starbucks would be perfect. That probably gave me fifteen to twenty minutes before Mom got here, but then the doorbell rang.

Damn. It was Veronica. She was early.

I rushed into the bathroom off the front hall and flipped on the light. The mirror confirmed what I'd suspected. My hair was going every which way but decent.

I splashed handfuls of water in my face and on my hair, patting it down, then dried it quickly with a hand towel. There wasn't anything I could do about the shirt. I hoped I didn't have BO. I chilled myself out and went to the door to let Veronica in, hoping I'd cleaned up enough.

We said our hellos, and soon she was taking Billy's vitals and handing me a fresh pair of latex gloves.

As I stepped closer to her, she looked me over and asked, "Did you get any sleep last night?"

Damn. Do I look that bad?

"I tried," I said. "I just couldn't."

She nodded. "You could probably get Billy's doctor to prescribe you some Ambien. That would help."

"Can't say that's really my style."

"A big glass of wine or a stiff cocktail can do the trick too."

"Not my style either."

"Oh, I didn't know—" she said, but I cut her off.

"It's okay. I'm just not a drinker. Never had a reason to start… and plenty not to." I'd seen the consequences of drinking throughout my life. First with Mom, then with Billy. While Mom had been able to stop, Billy's tastes, as I'd seen upstairs, had gotten far worse.

"I guess that would be true," Veronica said as she looked at Billy.

Veronica reached down and pulled the plastic tube out of the Prick's throat. This revealed a gaping hole sliced through his flesh and his windpipe. The hole was filled with yellowish-brown snot.

I pulled back involuntarily, again looking like a wuss. She'd seen it and there was no way to hide it or recover, so I kept my distance.

"That's nasty," I said.

"And that's why you need to clean his stoma twice a day."

"I didn't have to do it yesterday."

"After the catheter incident, I didn't want to put you through too much, so I did it myself."

"Thanks," I said.

Dammit. She totally thought I was a wuss.

Veronica pulled some gauze and cotton balls from her bag and handed them to me. I stepped closer to the bed and wiped the quarter-sized hole in Billy's throat with a strip of gauze. It felt so bizarre touching his neck when there was nothing there. My instinct was to close my eyes, but I opted to turn my head slightly, hoping she wouldn't notice this was totally grossing me out.

No such luck.

"Don't be dainty," she said. "You need to clean it out the best you can. If it's not cleaned properly, your brother could come down with pneumonia."

I forced myself to push deeper into the throat hole, wiping the snot out. Veronica stood directly across the bed from me. She watched my work closely.

"Good. That's better."

"If he can breathe on his own, how come they cut his neck open and put him on the ventilator?" I asked.

"It's difficult for comatose patients to support their own airways," she said. "This makes it easier for him to breathe."

"Gotcha." I didn't fully understand the medical reasons, but it still made sense. Nothing was ever easy when Billy was involved.

Next, Veronica lathered up Billy's scruffily bearded face and offered me the razor Mom had bought yesterday.

"You want to do the honors?" she asked.

"Can't say that's a good idea. Unless, of course, you want to risk me slipping and accidentally cutting the rest of his throat."

"You really don't care that much for your brother, do you?"

"We've had some issues."

"Such as?"

"I wouldn't even know where to start."

"The beginning's usually a good place."

"Well, the first thing I remember is back when I was five, Billy wanted to play with my G.I. Joe's I was already playing with—"

"G.I. Joe?"

"Hey, he was the real American hero. Anyway, Billy got mad that I wouldn't let him, so he pushed me. I fell right into the corner of the coffee table and got a trip to the emergency room and five stitches."

I pointed to the faint but still noticeable scar on the left side of my upper lip.

Veronica shrugged. "My sister and I gave each other more than our fair share of shiners and stitches growing up."

"Ever give each other new teeth?" I asked, tapping the veneers of my upper two front teeth.

"That we didn't," she said.

"Yeah, we were racing around our driveway on rollerblades. I was beating him good and naturally he didn't like that. So again, he pushed me. I broke the fall with my face and said adios to my two front teeth."

I thought that story might elicit some empathy from her. It didn't.

"Did he ever bean you in the head with anything?" she asked, turning Billy's head to reach the further part of his cheek with the razor.

"He threw a lot of things at me over the years, but I was pretty good at ducking."

"I wasn't," Veronica said. "My brother got mad at me and hit me in the head with a baseball once."

"Ouch."

"Yeah. I was out for about a minute. My mom was pretty scared. She really beat the crap out of him after I came to."

"At least your mom did that," I said. "All mine did was make him pretend to apologize and tell me to forgive him because he didn't really mean to hurt me."

"He probably didn't."

"Oh, I'm pretty sure he did."

"Sibling relationships can be challenging."

"Any of your siblings ever steal your car and total it?"

"Can't say that they did," she said, using my expression.

"At least I got you beat there."

I wasn't sure what else to say. I'd said more than I'd intended. These weren't things I wanted to think about, let alone discuss with anyone, especially Project Nurse. I had to figure a way out of this conversation. I took the easy route.

"I really need to go upstairs and grab a shower," I told her, and headed up the stairs.

20

A BETTER USE OF MY sleepless night would have been to scrub Billy's shower. In the middle of all that happened the day before, and the aggravations of the last night, I'd forgotten to scrub down the mold factory. There was no way I was getting in there. I found a washcloth, wet it, and used it to wash my face, pits, and crevices the best I could. I really would need to clean the shower sometime that day.

I checked Billy's medicine cabinet for some cologne and found a bottle of Eternity.

Eternity? Even with all of the money he had, the Prick still used Eternity? No wonder he had to settle for hookups with tattooed local skanks.

Still, I sprayed some on my neck and shirt. Eternity had been my go-to cologne in the 90s. Maybe it had some latent panty-dropper powers that would help me with Veronica.

As I got back downstairs, Mom came through the door carrying a large box from Yum Yum Donuts.

"Good morning," Mom said.

"Good morning," I replied as she handed me the box.

Yum Yum had always been my favorite. Especially when they were still hot and fresh in the morning.

"How's Billy doing today?" Mom asked Veronica.

"He's stable," Veronica said. "It doesn't seem like much has changed."

I knew it wasn't the news Mom wanted to hear, but she did her best to put it into a positive light.

"That's better than getting worse," Mom said as she bent down and kissed his recently shaved cheek. "Thank you for shaving him."

"You're welcome," Veronica said.

Mom came back over to me, opened the box of donuts I still held and picked out an old-fashioned strawberry that had always been her favorite.

Mom took a bite and turned to Veronica. "Now, be sure to grab yourself a donut before Danny eats them all."

"Thank you, but I've already had breakfast," Veronica said.

"But these are the best donuts in town," Mom said.

"I'm sure they're fantastic," Veronica said. "But I do need to stick to my training."

"One donut won't hurt you," Mom said while using a pinky finger to pluck a dangling piece of strawberry frosting from the corner of her mouth.

I decided to pile on. "I thought you runners needed your carbohydrates?"

The peer pressure was starting to get to Veronica. She looked me right in the eye and said, "Fine. I'll split one with you."

21

VERONICA WENT INTO THE KITCHEN with me. I cut a
Long John chocolate bar in half with a butter knife as she
pulled off her gloves and threw them in the trash. I put one
half of the Long John on a napkin for her, then took a bite
of my half. It was as good and delicious as I remembered,
especially since it was still pretty fresh. Veronica took a
slow, careful bite to avoid getting any crumbs or frosting
on her face or scrubs.

"Mmm. This is really good," she said.

"The best," I said with my mouth full of Long John.

She turned her back on me and walked over to the
sliding glass door, gazing out at the pool in the morning
light. "Your brother's got quite the place here," she said.

"It doesn't suck," I said, hoping to leave it at that.

Veronica unlatched the lock and pulled the handle
aside. She stepped out into the backyard, leaving the door
open. I decided that was my cue to follow her.

I joined Veronica standing at the edge of the pool's
entrance. She stared across the pool at the valley below.
The freeway could be seen in the distance, as the smog

wasn't too bad this early in the year.

"Billy seems to have done quite well for himself," she said.

"Believe it or don't."

She turned to me as she swallowed another bite of donut. "Sounds like there's a story there."

"Of course there is."

"'Kay. So how'd he make his money?"

"I'll give you three guesses."

She took a moment then said, "He invented a million-dollar app that keeps kids' faces glued to their phones."

"Survey says NEH. That would require both brains and motivation, two things he's never had."

"Hmm," she said. "He win a lawsuit against McDonald's for making his hot coffee too hot?"

"Survey says NEH. But that was a worthy guess. I could see him doing that."

"Then he must have answered one of those emails from a Nigerian prince asking for help to move his money to America and it turned out to be real?"

"Now that was really close, but NEH."

"Algerian prince, then?"

"Yeah, one named Prince Super Lotto."

"Seriously?"

"Yep. Dumbass hit the Lotto."

"You're BSing me."

"I would never lie to a woman sharing a chocolate donut with me."

"Actually, I think you would."

"Possibly. But in this case, I'm not. A few years ago, Billy was unemployed—as usual—and living with my mom. He'd wrecked his car in a DUI, so he walked to the store, bought some beer, some dip, and a lottery ticket, and bam, he hit ye old jackpot."

"That's one way to do it."

"Yeah, while the rest of us bust our asses, the jobless wonder buys a lottery ticket with money he likely stole from my mom, and next thing you know, Jed's a millionaire."

"With a major prescription drug problem," Veronica said.

It shocked me to hear her say that. No one in the family ever would admit that fact. Even though they all knew it, I was the only one who would ever say it out loud.

"Yeah," I said. "Heck of a combination."

"It's good he didn't blow it. He'd never be able to afford the type of care you're giving him."

"Well, that's where dumb luck comes in again. I guess the jackass didn't realize that when he bought the ticket, he'd agreed to take the money in monthly installments for twenty years. If he'd had it all at once, it would be gone. That I can guarantee."

She studied me then said, "As much as you don't like your brother, it's hard for me to understand why he named you as his agent."

"That's an easy one. He hates me just as much."

Oops!

I should've lied and said I didn't know. Revealing the true depths of my disdain for the Prick wouldn't help me get the scrubs off of Project Nurse. No one in their right mind was supposed to loathe their brother in a coma—even with all the crap he'd pulled.

"Mom seems to have forgotten my coffee, so I need to get something to wash this down," I said, and went back into the house.

I couldn't believe how much I'd said to Veronica. I needed to be more careful. I only had nine days left to close the deal. Showing a bit of vulnerability would probably help. But letting her really know how much I hated the Prick would sink any chances I had of breaking every single one of her rules.

Little could I have expected that it would be Dad who helped me make some serious progress in that regard.

22

WHEN DAD ARRIVED SLIGHTLY BEFORE noon, I wasn't the only one who couldn't stop staring at him.

Not only was he plugging a black Stratocaster into a small amp he'd already plugged into a wall, but also he looked different. Really different. Since leaving last night, he'd dyed his damn hair. It was brown now. And not the proper shade of brown it should have been, but a dark brown that screamed, *I use Just for Men.*

"What are you doing?" I asked Dad, unable to take my eyes off his hair.

Mom answered me before he could. "I told him not to, but you know how much he listens to me."

I wasn't sure if she was talking about his hair or the guitar and amp.

Dad ignored Mom and said, "This place could use a little livening up. And what livens things up better than some good old rock and roll?"

"I don't think that's a good idea," I said.

"Neither do I," Mom agreed.

When Veronica came out of the bathroom, her eyes

immediately went to Dad's darker shade of hair. I saw a touch of a grin at the corners of her mouth, but she quickly recovered and returned to her solid professional expression. "What's going on here?" she asked, pointing at the amp.

"Dad wants to put on a rock show for your patient," I said.

Mom said, "Please tell him this is a bad idea."

"Actually," Veronica said, "music's good for comatose patients. It's been shown to stimulate brain activity in a number of them."

Great. Rather than giving us a solid majority against Dad, she'd shut me and Mom down.

"See?" Dad said. "I'm helping."

Dad strummed the guitar. It sounded good. But I still didn't want him to play.

"What would you like to hear?" Dad asked Veronica.

"Why don't you play something Billy would like?" she said, giving the safe answer.

"Yeah," I said. "Know any Snoop Dogg?"

"Why the hell would I?" Dad asked.

That didn't tweak him enough, so I dropped the A-bomb on him. "Then how about some Bee Gees?"

"You know better than to go there with me."

I smiled at Dad, knowing I'd scored a direct hit. But Veronica prevented me from enjoying it for more than a moment when she said, "Why don't you play one of *your* favorites, then?"

Dad smiled widely at her. "That I can do."

Without hesitation, Dad broke into the opening riff of "Layla." It's a great song, and he'd been playing it for as long as I could remember. It impressed me that his playing remained top-notch. He'd let so many things in his life go, but when it came to picking a guitar, he definitely hadn't let that ability get away from him.

Unfortunately, when he opened his mouth to sing, it all fell apart. The years had not been kind to Dad's vocal cords. Now his vocal cords weren't being kind to us.

I did my best to ignore him by turning to Billy and seeing how I might be able to help Veronica. She hid it much better than I ever could have, but the look she gave told me that the feline strangling session Dad had commenced grated on her ears too. Lucky for us, he had only plugged the guitar into his amp and hadn't brought along a mic.

I looked down at Billy. Dad's singing might've qualified as awful enough to raise the dead or comatose. Maybe this would do the trick to revive the Prick.

Without warning, the sound of the guitar quieted and we were left with Dad's shrieking vocals. The amp had somehow lost power.

I turned around to find Dad pointing a finger at Mom. "What did you do that for?"

Mom stood behind the amp. The electrical cord had come out of the wall and now lay limp on the floor.

"I didn't do anything," Mom said. "Well, not on purpose."

"There's no way you could've missed the cord," Dad said.

"You never should have put it where people walk," Mom retorted, and off to the fights my parents went.

Dad yelled, "You don't have the right to come up in the middle of my song and unplug me."

"It was an accident. I tripped."

"That's very convenient timing for an accident."

"If I'd pulled the plug on purpose, I'd gladly tell you that was the case."

"I seriously doubt that."

"I'm not the woman you were married to. I don't hide from the truth anymore. I embrace it and speak it boldly."

"Then why won't you admit that you tripped on purpose?"

I couldn't take it anymore and stepped in between them. "Are you two really going to do this crap every day?" I asked them.

Mom and Dad looked at me like I had accused them both of committing murder.

"You were standing right here, Danny Boy," Dad said. "You saw how she started it."

"You want to see me start something with you, James?" Mom said. "I'd be more than happy to."

"You see what I have to deal with from her?" Dad said to me.

"And what do you think about what I've had to deal with from you?"

"Stop. Both of you," I said. "I'm the one who's got the most to deal with here, and I really don't want to listen to any of this. Okay?"

My parents stared at me in disbelief.

Finally, Mom nodded. "You're absolutely right," she said, then looked to Dad. "You should leave."

"Why do I have to leave?" he asked.

"Because if you'd been any kind of a father, Billy wouldn't be here like this."

"He didn't learn to get loaded from watching me," Dad fired back. That shot hurt Mom. She gritted her teeth and was about to go for his jugular.

I blocked Mom's path, standing before her and putting my hands up to keep her from getting to Dad.

"I'm not doing this anymore," I said. "If you two are going to act like this, I can't have you both here at the same time."

"You see?" Mom said, looking around me to Dad. "You do need to leave."

"But you're the one who started it!" Dad said.

"Shut up!" I screamed.

The room went silent.

Mom stared at me. "Don't you raise your voice to me."

I took three deep breaths. I needed to calm down. I didn't need to get drawn into this, but I couldn't handle their incessant arguing anymore. Tina's plan for keeping Billy and me apart when Mom had her heart attack came back to my mind.

"Here's how it's going to work," I said. "Mom, you're much more of a morning person, so you can come over and see Billy in the mornings. Dad, the afternoons are yours."

"You're giving us visitation hours?" Mom said.

"If I'm going to keep my sanity, I have to."

My parents were quiet as they worked things out in their minds. They could see I was serious and didn't want to push it any further.

"What about the evenings?" Mom asked.

"I don't know," I said. I hadn't factored that in but quickly made a decision. "You can alternate. You have the even days, and Dad has the odd ones."

I could see Dad checking his watch in my peripheral vision.

"Well, it's now twelve oh six," he said, looking at Mom with a wicked little grin. "I guess you'll be leaving."

"This starts today?" Mom asked. I could see the mixture of disbelief and desperation in her eyes. She didn't want to be kept away from Billy. I momentarily considered reneging on my decision, but I couldn't.

Taking care of Billy was maximizing my stress level. Layering Mom and Dad's never-ending arguments on top of that was just too much.

I looked down when I told her, "I'm afraid it has to."

Mom didn't like the answer, but thankfully she decided not to battle me over it.

"Fine," she said, gripping the strap of her oxygen machine tightly. Mom went around me and over to Billy's bed. She kissed his cheek and stroked his hair.

I looked back at Veronica. She pretended to be occupied tending to Billy, but I knew she'd taken in the whole thing. I'd probably lost a lot of points in her eyes, but I couldn't put up with these two anymore. I just couldn't.

Mom turned away from Billy then, and without saying a single thing or even giving me a passing glance, walked to the front door and left.

Dad smiled and plugged his amplifier back into the wall. I went after Mom.

23

"THANKS FOR NOT MAKING THIS harder than it already is," I said to Mom as we reached her Lexus.

"Of course," she said, opening her car door. "That's what your father's for." Mom got in behind the wheel.

"You okay?" I asked, looking down at her through the open door.

"I'll be fine," Mom said, giving me a weak smile. "I should go to a meeting anyway."

"I didn't know you still went to them."

"It's not like you ever get cured," she said.

Damn. Had I accidentally just thrown my mother off the wagon?

Mom must've picked up on my thoughts. "Don't worry," she said. "It's been almost ten years since I've had a drink of anything. I'm fine."

"Okay."

"Are you?"

"Ask me later. I still gotta go back in there and be stuck with Dad."

"You're the one who set the visitation schedule."

She was right. I knew it was another attempt to get me to scrap it, but Mom also knew I wouldn't.

"I think Veronica's sweet on you," Mom said. "And she's single."

"I'll see you tonight, Mom," I said, and closed the car door for her.

Mom drove off to her AA meeting and I went back inside. From the doorway, I could hear Dad say, "The Eagles were the best. No one else has ever come close."

"My brother and I saw them a few years ago," Veronica said. "They really put on a great show."

"You should've seen them back in the day," Dad said. "When they were hungry and making a name for themselves. That was when they were the best. I got to jam with them one night after a gig they did at the Troubadour."

"That must've been exciting."

"Oh, it was. If only that damn Felder hadn't gone and screwed it all up," Dad said, then came out of his reminiscing and asked her, "What's your favorite Eagles song?"

I intervened on behalf of everyone with decent hearing in the house. "Dad, why don't we give the music a bit of a break?"

"I didn't even get to finish one song. Besides, you heard Veronica. Music's good for Billy."

"Can't say it's doing anything for the rest of us."

"You're just jealous," Dad said.

"Jealous of what?" *You getting with Veronica? That'll never happen.*

"That I'm a better player than you."

"Yeah, that must be it."

"Hold on," Veronica said to me. "You play too?"

Dad answered for me. "Does he play? He's the only one of my kids who ever did anything with music. He could've been one of the greatest rock and roll guitarists ever. But what does he do? He decides to play country."

"I love country," she said.

Ha! Take that, Dad.

"Nobody's perfect," he said, looking downcast.

Veronica's eyes were now on me. "Play us a song."

Yes!

Dad's scheme had boomeranged into my favor. I was regaining points I might have lost a little while ago. And Veronica's rule continued to crumble. I'd long known that anytime a woman wanted you to play for her, she also wanted you to play *with* her.

Still, I couldn't appear too eager.

"I doubt I know anything Billy would like either," I said. Truthfully, I didn't.

She kept her eyes fixed on me and said, "Then play something for me."

Bingo.

I stepped over to Dad, opening my hands to take the Strat from him.

"May I?" I asked.

Dad didn't want to give the instrument up, but probably knew he'd come off as a total jerk if he didn't. He let his reluctance drop and handed me his Strat.

I strummed it a couple times even though I already knew it was in tune.

"What do you want to hear?" I asked Veronica.

"You know any Brad Paisley songs?"

Riiiigght.

Of all the country artists she could have requested me to cover, she had to pick Brad. Why him? That was completely unfair, but I should've known that was how it would turn out. Billy was in the room. Even comatose, his presence continued to play havoc with my happiness.

I couldn't tell Veronica that the request list was already full, like I did when people requested a Paisley tune in a club. Nor could I say I didn't know any of his songs. She wouldn't buy it. Even if she did, it would wreck the momentum I had going with her.

"Then you'll probably know this one," I told Veronica, and started playing.

If I had to play a Brad Paisley song for Project Nurse, then why not "Ticks"? It was not only an excellent song, but it contained plenty of double meanings about two people getting naked together, all in the interest of health and hygiene. That had to appeal to a medical professional on a subliminal, sexual level.

And from what I could tell, it was working.

Not once during the song did Veronica break eye

contact with me. She wasn't embarrassed and she wasn't offended. Project Nurse was in my zone, which was a very dangerous place for her to be, but a very good one for me.

I wrapped up the song, Veronica smiled and nodded her appreciation. "Nice choice," she said. "For an exotic dancer, you're quite the musician."

"It helps me cover the shortfall when my G-string's a little light on tips."

She laughed. Major progress had been made. Dad could obviously see that the flirtation between Veronica and me had escalated nicely. He snatched the guitar out of my hands.

"I'll never play that country crap," Dad said to her, "But Southern rock, I'll play all night long."

Dad instantly broke into "Sweet Home Alabama," trying to steer Veronica's attention back to him. It didn't matter. Her eyes remained connected to me, especially when he started to sing.

I stepped closer to Veronica.

"I should've known you were a musician," she said.

"Yeah?"

"Yeah. You have the attitude."

"I hope that's a compliment."

"It is."

The door had opened wider. I couldn't let it close and took a bold step forward. "Well," I said, "if you ever need someone to check you for ticks, chiggers, skin cancer, or anything else, all you have to do is let me know."

Veronica shook her head but was still smiling. "I'll give you this. You're persistent."

"My dad always told me that if a girl says no seventeen times, she really means yes."

"You're far from seventeen. I've only had to shoot you down two or three so far."

"As long as I'm making progress."

Veronica looked down at my motionless brother in his bed. "Billy, I hope you come around soon to save me from these two."

Ouch!

Had she really just lumped in my efforts to get her out of her scrubs with my Dad's lounge-lizard tactics?

Dammit!

Project Nurse might take a little more time than I'd figured.

24

BIG PAUL CALLED ME THAT afternoon.

He asked about Billy, and I told him what everyone kept telling me—it was a wait-and-see kind of thing. I quickly switched topics and asked him, "So how'd Rusty do?"

"Pretty damn good," Paul said. "The kid's really got talent."

"Well, that's why I hired him."

"Yeah, I know, but seriously, Danny, he's really got it. I wouldn't be surprised if he decided to put his own band together."

"Well, don't let him hear you say that. Rusty's sly enough to threaten that to get a bigger cut of the take."

"I know. I just wanted to make sure you knew."

"I appreciate it. I'll be back in a week. That should keep his time as the frontman from getting to his head too much."

Big Paul and I said our goodbyes, and he offered his best wishes for Billy. I considered going back downstairs and working on Project Nurse a bit more. But that would mean I'd have to submit to the torture of Dad's one-man Southern rock revue. Besides, I needed to get the full scrub-down of Billy's shower out of the way.

I grabbed the cleaning supplies I needed and began the decontamination project.

I'd worked up quite a sweat removing the mold and mildew when I heard Sergio's voice behind me. "You're right. She's quite the looker."

I looked over my shoulder to see my former drummer standing in the doorway between Billy's bedroom and the bathroom.

"That's pretty scandalous coming from a pastor and a married man."

"I wasn't undressing her with my eyes," Serg said. "I was more curious to see if your tastes have held up."

"Now, you've seen the proof that they have."

"Don't think I ever recall you going for less than a seven and a half."

"That's where not drinking helps. I've never had to deal with the consequences of a beer goggles hookup."

Sergio winced. My comment likely had pulled up an unpleasant memory or two in his head. "You were definitely smarter than the rest of us," he said.

"I'm not so sure about that," I said, and went back to scrubbing the shower.

"Yeah," Sergio said. "I heard you ran into her."

That stopped my scrubbing.

"Bad news still travels too fast in Norco," I said.

"I doubt that many people know."

"Well, you seem to."

"Only because Tina told me."

"That figures."

"It's not Tina's fault. I texted her to ask how Billy was doing and if you needed anything."

I turned back to Sergio. "And she told you about my run-in at Target."

"She said she was concerned about you."

"I'm sure she did."

We were silent for a moment, then Serg said, "It could've been worse."

"Can't say how that'd be possible."

"You could've run into Lonnie."

Oh yeah, Lonnie. My former bass player. "He's still pissed at me, huh?"

"Any time I've mentioned your name in front of him, he goes off for at least an hour about how you royally screwed him."

"Don't you mean how I royally screwed you, as in both of you?"

Sergio looked at me intensely. I was ready for him to finally let me have it. But he didn't.

"You know," he said, "I was mad at you at first, but you did what you thought you had to do. You had a shot and you took it. I can't begrudge you that."

"Can't say that worked out so well."

"Nashville's a tough business."

"I think *brutal* is a better word."

"It probably is. But Vegas is treating you good, right?"

"Yeah. I've got a solid group and I found this fiddle player we would've killed to have back in the day."

"That sounds good. How's the writing going?"

Why'd he need to ask that?

That was the one thing I didn't want to talk about. I didn't want to lie to Sergio, so I went for the best brush-off I could come up with.

"Eh. You know."

"No, I'm not exactly sure what that means."

I didn't want to elaborate. The best course of action was to remain silent.

"Danny, you're still writing... right?"

I stayed quiet.

"Aren't you?" he said. Sergio wasn't going to let it go, but I could tell it wasn't malicious. He was genuinely curious, and his tone carried a notch of concern. Still, I couldn't bring myself to utter a sound.

I simply shook my head.

Sergio took a step back and exhaled a long breath he'd been holding. My answer shocked him. "Wow. I can't imagine you not writing songs."

"There's been a lot of shit in my life I wouldn't have imagined. Yet here I am taking care of the Prick behind most of it. How's that for reverse karma, Mr. Preacher?"

"Karma isn't quite in the Bible."

"That's fine. I'm not really a fan of either."

"Well, hey, I just wanted to stop in and see how you're doing."

"Yeah. I'm fine, but I've really got to get this shower clean if I want to use it."

I turned my back on Sergio and gave my full attention to the shower.

He didn't say anything else. When I looked over my shoulder a couple of minutes later, I was relived to find that he'd left.

25

"GOOD?" MOM ASKED ME AS I devoured my third slice of meatloaf while she still worked on her first piece at a more refined pace.

I was pretty sure she already knew the answer to her question and was looking for some validation. Every time I came home to see her, she made me meatloaf, and I never complained. It was my number one comfort food. Boy, did I need it now.

True to her word, Mom had returned to Billy's at five p.m. I had to usher Dad out, which was made easier by the fact that Veronica was also leaving. With Dad and Veronica heading to their cars at the same time, I lost the ability to walk her out again.

But as the famous show tune said, there'd always be tomorrow. At that moment, however, there was meatloaf.

Since Mom needed the validation, and I genuinely loved her meatloaf, I said, "I can get just about any kind of food in Vegas, but I have yet to find a place that can make meatloaf like you can."

Mom's wide smile told me that my answer delighted

her.

It also proved to be a mistake.

"I can give you the recipe if you'd like," she said.

"I'm not much of a cook."

"You should take the time to learn. Women love a man who can cook."

Here we go again.

I shoveled a huge chunk of meatloaf into my mouth, hoping that would stop this line of conversation. No such luck.

"I'm sure Veronica would find that quite attractive," Mom said.

I swallowed and said, "You know, I don't need you to play matchmaker for me."

"I don't have a clue why you'd say that," Mom said, acting as if she was innocent.

The alarm let out its triple beep, and I next heard Tina at the front door saying, "Hello?"

"Back here," I said.

A few seconds later, Tina entered the kitchen then joined us in the dining area. In one hand, she carried her briefcase. In the other was her laptop case.

"How's Billy today?" Tina asked as she put her things down and took the seat at my right hand and across from Mom.

"Still comatose," I said.

Tina gave me a dissatisfied face and said, "This isn't something to joke about."

"You never have gotten my sense of humor."

Before Tina could continue to state her displeasure, Mom said, "Grab yourself a plate. There's plenty here."

Tina stared at the wonderful half-eaten loaf of meat with outright disgust. You'd have thought it was a steaming turd sitting on the plate instead of the product of Mom's best cooking.

"How many times do I need to remind you how dangerous red meat is?" she asked Mom.

Mom gave no ground. "It's one of the few vices I still have, and I don't plan on giving it up."

"You should," Tina said. "The consumption of red meat is the number one cause of heart disease, and research shows that it's linked to cancer."

"When did you become a vegetarian?" I asked. At no time when we were growing up did I ever remember Tina turning down a Double Double at In-N-Out.

"After her heart attack," Tina said. "And I'm vegan, by the way."

"So it's even worse," I said.

"I've never been healthier," Tina said. "And with heart disease running in our family, you should consider putting yourself on a plant-based diet."

"And I wonder why you never married," Mom said.

Tina glared at her. "What's that supposed to mean?"

"Honey, if you want to catch a husband, he needs to know you can satisfy him whenever he's hungry or horny."

"Mom!" Tina said.

I laughed and said to my sister, "She really has a knack for TMI these days, doesn't she?"

Tina ignored my remark and kept her focus on Mom. "My decision not to include any animal products in my diet in no way hampers my prospects for marriage."

"Actually, it might," I said. "No real man is going to want tofu."

Tina whipped her head in my direction. "There are plenty of real men that care for their health and don't crave a bloody steak."

"When's the last time one took you out for a garden burger?" I asked.

"I don't see you with any prospects for the altar either," Tina said.

Damn lawyers.

Before I could think up something more cutting as a reply, Mom did the job for me.

"Tina, Danny's clock's not running out of ticks."

"Mother!" Tina shouted. I couldn't tell if Tina's indignation was authentic or dramatized. Either way, I enjoyed it.

Mom continued, "All I'm saying is if you're going to give me a grandchild, you really should get on with it."

"You already have a grandchild," Tina said.

"It would be nice to have more," Mom said, then looked at me and added, "From both of you."

I put my attention back on to my plate but found I no

longer had an appetite since Tina had mentioned the Kid.

"Thanks for making dinner, Mom," I said. "I'm stuffed."

"Of course. Anytime, Danny," Mom said.

I stood and picked up my plate as I pushed my chair back. I needed to get out of there.

"And since we're on the topic of grandchildren," Mom said, "Jessie would like to bring Mason by to see his father."

"That's not happening," I said, turning my back on both of them and taking my plate over to the kitchen sink.

"And why not?" Mom asked.

"Because I said it's not."

Tina jumped in. "You can't tell them they can't come over?"

I locked eyes with my sister. "Oh, yes I can. I'm in charge. Remember?"

"Danny," Mom said. "Don't you think it's time to let those things from the past go?"

"This isn't about the past," I said. "It's about right here and now. And neither Jessie nor that kid are stepping a single toe into this house while I'm here."

"Hmmm. That could work," Mom said.

"What could?" I had no idea what she meant.

"You could go for a drive or a walk and Jessie could bring Mason over while you're gone."

"No. That's not going to work because that's not what I meant. If either of them come over here, whether I'm here or not, then I'm going back to Vegas."

"Don't be ridiculous," Tina said.

"I'm not. I'm being in charge."

"Danny," Mom said. "Jessie came to the hospital to see Billy every day he was there."

"Well, this ain't the hospital."

"Mason really wants to see his father."

"I don't care. It's not gonna happen. And this conversation is over."

I dumped the rest of the partially eaten slice of meatloaf into the garbage can and set the plate in the sink. I'd rather be sitting in the silence next to the Prick than sitting in here getting badgered by these two.

But I still had more say to Mom and Tina. "And before you both start conspiring on how to trick me into changing my mind, I'm warning you, don't even try or I'm gone."

"Don't you talk to me that way," Mom said.

"Then keep them away from here, 'cause I don't want anything to do with her or the Kid."

"If that's the case," Tina said, "you should start praying when Sergio comes over."

"What are you getting at?" I asked.

Tina took her time to answer, clearly enjoying this. "Well, if Billy doesn't recover, you're going to be dealing with Mason for quite some time."

I took a step closer to Tina, my fists clenching as I did. "The hell I am."

With a condescending look, Tina asked, "You didn't read the whole trust, did you?"

26

"THIS IS ABSOLUTE BULLSHIT," I said, pushing Billy's trust over his prone body and back to Tina.

She took it and said matter-of-factly, "It's what Billy wants."

"Which clarifies that it's bullshit."

Besides naming me as the agent for all his medical decisions, the Prick put all of his money and everything he owned into a trust. In the event of his death, everything would go to the Kid. But not immediately. On the Kid's twenty-first birthday. Until that time, it would be my responsibility to manage everything.

If Billy died, I was legally tied to his kid for another ten years.

Ten years? Uh-uh.

Billy was lucky I'd given him ten days.

"No way," I said. "This medical directive was enough. I'm not taking care of anything else."

"I understand," Tina said. "And I think it won't be too hard to get you out of it."

"It better not be."

"Given that everything goes to Mason, I'm sure the court wouldn't have a problem substituting Jessie as the trustee."

"I told you not to mention that slut's name in front of me."

"Don't call her that," Mom yelled at me from the kitchen, where she was cleaning the dishes.

I wanted to yell back at her that that's exactly what Jessie was, but didn't.

Tina leaned in closer to me. "Regardless of how you feel about Jessie, it's no reason for you to be mean to Mason. He's innocent in all of this."

"If he's Billy's kid, then I promise you, he's anything but innocent."

"There's no use talking to you, is there?"

"No, there's not."

27

W<small>HY COULDN'T</small> I <small>SLEEP</small>?

I was now running on three days without a single minute of REM. I couldn't focus. My mind refused to concentrate on anything. Other than the fact that my brother was indeed the biggest prick on planet Earth, that was. Everything was his fault.

It was his fault I was here. It was his fault I hadn't slept in three days. It was his fault I hadn't been laid once during that time.

Holy shit. Was that it?

Was it the lack of sex that was really keeping me from sleeping? Was it really such a part of my routine that I couldn't function normally when I wasn't getting any on a regular basis?

It had been so long since I'd had a gap between projects that I wasn't sure. True, having to deal with Billy, my family, and the assorted crap that accompanied all of that probably wasn't helping. But I'd been dealing with that as long as I'd been alive. Not knocking boots with a female of our species in a week was unusual for me.

I had to do something, and the something I had to do, I hadn't done in a long, long time. I wasn't sure I could. Not that I'd forgotten how. Once puberty hits and you learn how to pleasure yourself, you don't forget. I'd just weaned myself off it when I learned that even halfway-talented musicians can always get girls. And I was more than halfway talented.

The thought of pulling up some porn on my phone momentarily ran through my mind. It wasn't really an option. Unlike most men my age, I wasn't a fan of pornography. Not for any moral reasons or some self-righteous crap like that. I'd just always thought of sex like sports. If I'm not a participant, I really don't care to watch.

Besides, I had a pretty decent imagination.

I started off thinking about Project Nurse. Oh yeah, Veronica would be a lot of fun to get into bed. But I couldn't hold her image in my mind. I thought back a few nights to Project Redhead and the bliss we could have enjoyed, but I kept seeing Rusty's bearded face in my minds eye. Even in my fantasies he was stealing her from me.

What the hell is wrong with me?

I took a deep breath and imagined myself back in the bedroom of my youth in the house on Center Street late at night. I could see my teenage self taking myself in my left hand while holding the one *Playboy* I owned in my right. It was open to the centerfold. Sergio and Lonnie had given the magazine to me as a gift on my sixteenth birthday.

The pictorial images of Miss January 1997 somehow came out of the indecent scrapbooks of my mind. Jami Ferrell. She'd been the ideal woman to me. Oh, how many times we'd had incredible imaginary sex. And here we were again after all these years. Together in bed just like old times.

I've never been the one to get past second base and tell, so I'll leave it at this: Jami still knew how to make me quite happy in the sexual adventures of my mind. As I dozed off, imagining her perfect body happily snoozing against mine, I realized Jami had to be in her forties by this point in time.

I bet she still has an amazing bod.

Hmmm. Older women can be fun.

Maybe Jami's single and likes country music.

PART III

Family Feuding

1

AFTER GETTING MY FIRST SOLID night's sleep after seventy-two hours and my first sexual release in a week, you'd think I'd be refreshed and energized the next morning. That wasn't the case. While the physical exhaustion was gone and I wasn't necessarily tired, I didn't want to get out of bed on Wednesday morning. I wanted to stay there as long as possible, but that wasn't in the cards.

Ten days. I only had to stay for ten days—and two were already done. Only eight to go. Billy had a week plus a day to show some signs of improvement. If that didn't happen... Well, I didn't want to think about that. Billy had eight days.

Eight damn days.

That would be a long stretch for me, but doable.

In hindsight, something strange happened during those eight days. And not with Billy. With me. A routine of sorts developed for me. Somehow I slipped into this new flow of things without even realizing it at the time.

Five mornings a week, Veronica would come in at nine. Mom would show up soon after trying to force-feed us ten thousand calories of something. Afternoons became the Pathetic Pickup Attempt Show starring Dad. He tried everything he had. He attempted to impress Veronica with stories of great rockers he once jammed with after parties in Hollywood. But the name-dropping wasn't working for him.

Aunt Geena and Uncle Jimmy drove in from Arizona that weekend. She and Mom would sit at Billy's bedside and talk about anything and everything. Uncle Jimmy would plant himself in front of the TV. When Dad's time started, Mom and Aunt Geena would leave to shop or grab lunch or who knows what. Uncle Jimmy would sit with Dad. Dad would talk to him nonstop. Uncle Jimmy would nod his response, either not able to or not wanting to contribute to the conversation. It was a good bet he'd turned down his Miracle Ear.

Tina came over every evening after her days of providing justice to the community. She spent most of the weekends at Billy's too. Usually, she had work to do for a trial. And of course Sergio would swing by from time to time. They'd pray for Billy and I'd go take a walk. I needed to get out and have some fresh air. Well, as fresh as it can get in Southern California. I just didn't need to be around the whole praying thing.

The bright side to all of this was Veronica. We developed quite a rapport. Each day that went by, I figured the next would be the one where I'd wind up removing her bra with my teeth. Unfortunately, she held fast to her rule.

And I let mine slip.

When day ten arrived, and Billy wasn't getting any better, for some unknown reason, I decided to give it another five days.

At the end of that time, Veronica and I had grown a lot closer personally. Unfortunately, we had not moved any closer to a firm mattress or nearby sofa. Still, something was happening between us, but again not with Billy. I decided to give it five more days again.

Before I knew what had happened, I'd been staying in Norco taking care of the Prick for thirty days. An entire month of my life had disappeared—and during that time I hadn't seen so much as a bare shoulder from Veronica. That likely meant whatever was going to happen had already happened.

Yet I enjoyed the time I spent with her immensely. I had to wonder if she and I were becoming friends.

I hoped not, as that would be a death sentence for any sexual escapades between us. Hence why I never allowed myself to be friends with any women I found attractive. The friend zone was for losers. But had I accidentally allowed myself to wind up there Veronica? I hoped not but wasn't sure.

However, there was one thing I was sure about.

Billy wasn't getting better.

He'd been in a coma for thirty-seven days and his condition hadn't changed at all. Well, it had, but the changes were not positive.

He looked like absolute crap. Despite bringing him home, hiring Veronica to help care for him, and all the prayers Sergio and everyone else were saying for him, Billy wasn't showing any signs of life other than what the machines were providing for him.

I'd thought the worst thing I'd be faced with was convincing Mom that Billy belonged in a nursing home. But if Mom wouldn't let me put him in a home where he'd get real care, how in the hell would I ever convince her that pulling the plug would be the right thing?

I needed the assistance of the most manipulative person I'd ever known. If she couldn't help me make the case without sending Mom into full arrest or a month in rehab, no one could.

I hated to admit it, but I needed the help of my sister.

2

"WE'VE GOT TO FIGURE OUT what we're going to say to Mom," I told Tina.

"About what?" Tina said without looking up at me from the comfy chair that she'd made her evening workstation the past month.

I'd waited until she and I were alone together. Dad had watched TV and left for the night. Now it was only the two of us alone in the living room with Billy, his bed, and the machines keeping him alive.

"About Billy."

"Okay. And?" She looked up at me and appeared genuinely clueless about what I was getting at.

"I've been here a month now. The accident was thirty-seven days ago."

"I hadn't realized it," she said, standing and going to Billy's bedside. "Every day I come by, I think I'm going to walk in and find him sitting up and cracking jokes."

I paused before speaking, then finally said what I had to: "I can't say that looks like it's gonna happen."

She turned to me. There was fear in her eyes.

"You're actually considering turning off his life support."

Her words made me feel guilty. I had to respond. "I'm not considering anything. You've read his trust. It's what he wants."

"Let's give it another week or so."

"Is another week or more really going to matter?"

"It might be all he needs to recover."

"When I first got here, you said he probably only needed another week. I thought you might be right. I gave him that... then more. But look at him. He hasn't improved at all. If anything, he's starting to look a lot less like himself."

"He just needs more time."

"I really don't know about that."

"Sometimes it takes people years to recover."

"Well, I don't have years," I blurted out. "I've got a band and a life to get back."

"So you're only concerned with getting back to your music," she said.

"Can you stop being a lawyer and twisting my words for one minute? Billy's trust is clear. If he's not going to recover to how he was before the accident, he doesn't want to be kept alive. Not like this."

Tina's next words knocked me back.

"Then you're willing to send him to hell just like that?"

"What are you talking about?"

"Look at all the bad things Billy's done in his life."

"I've been on the receiving end of more than my fair share of them."

"Right. And if Billy dies now without repenting for what he's done, he's going to be damned."

"Hey, that's not my problem. I'm only responsible for doing what he said he wanted done in his stupid trust."

Tina's expression instantly contorted into her meanest bitch face.

"I should've known," she said like a cobra spitting venom at me.

"Known what?"

"You only stayed so you could you kill him."

"Kill him? I didn't get him high and put him behind the wheel. He did that all on his own."

"But this is the next best thing, isn't it? You can just nonchalantly end Billy's life while saying you were just following his wishes. That's why you really agreed to take care of him. That's why you stayed as long as you have."

"I'm here because you conned me into it because of Mom's health."

"That's a good story, but you could have easily let Dad take care of him, but you didn't. This way everyone would think that you're a good brother and never suspect that the real reason you pulled the plug on him was to finally get your revenge on Billy for stealing Jessie from you."

"You're absolutely insane."

Tina turned her back on me and began packing up her

laptop and case files.

"I prosecute people for a living," she said. "I recognize an ulterior motive when I see it."

"You've really losing it."

"No, you're the one who's losing it." Tina stood with her things. "I'm filing an injunction against you in the morning. You're not turning off these machines."

"It's what Billy wants!"

"Billy made a lot of bad decisions in his life. One of them was naming you as his trustee. It's a good thing I'm here to help him fix that mistake."

Tina pushed past me and out the front door.

Am I the only sane one left in this family?

3

TINA MOVED QUICKLY TO PROVE she hadn't been bluffing.

When I was taking the trash cans out to the curb that next afternoon, I heard a man ask from behind me, "Excuse me. Are you Daniel Meacham?"

My senses immediately went on high alert. No one ever called me by my proper name. It was Danny, Danny Mack, Danny Boy, occasionally Dan, but seldom if ever Daniel. Even Mom, when she got mad, threw in my middle name and called me Daniel James. It was probably easier for her to conjure more anger if she included Dad's name. If someone was asking for me as Daniel, they didn't know me.

I turned from the trash cans to see a man in his mid-twenties, almost half a foot taller than me and as skinny as could be, walk across the street. A car was parked over there with an open door. Had he been sitting there watching me? Had he been waiting for me?

"What if I am?" I wasn't in the mood for anyone's crap.

Skinny Bones Jones pulled a sheaf of paper that had

been folded three ways out of a back pocket and offered it to me. I didn't even consider reaching for it.

Before I could ask what it might be, he told me.

"This is a summons for you to appear in court. There's also a temporary restraining order in place to prevent you from taking any action to terminate life support for one William Meacham."

"Of course there is," I said, and took the papers from him.

He turned and left, not saying anything obnoxious or pretending to be kind. I didn't blame him. He was just doing his job. Like I was trying to do the one my prick brother had thrust on me.

I unfolded the document and verified that Christina Lynne Meacham had indeed launched the legal attack against me she'd threatened the night before. I'd never doubted that she would. She'd tricked me into staying to take care of Billy despite every instinct within me saying to hightail it back to Vegas. It hadn't been about Mom's stress level. It had always been about Tina having her way, despite what Billy had put in his trust.

I walked back into the house. Mom was at Billy's bed with Veronica. I thought about pulling Mom into the kitchen to talk but didn't see the point. Veronica had seen enough to know how screwed up this family was.

"Well, your daughter is officially and certifiably nuts," I said as I shut the door.

"What did Tina do now?" Mom asked.

I held up the summons. "She's trying to get me removed as Billy's agent."

"Why would she do that?"

I looked down at my shoes. Unsure how to proceed after my face-off with Tina, I hadn't raised the issue with Mom.

"Because…" I started, but couldn't continue.

"You want to turn the machines off," Mom finished for me.

"It's what Billy wants," I said as if apologizing, even though I had nothing to apologize for.

Mom nodded and went into the kitchen. I looked at Veronica. There was a compassionate look on her face, but she didn't say a word. I decided to follow after Mom.

"Mom…" I said as I came into the kitchen.

"There's no need to explain. Billy chose you because he knew you'd do what he asked you to do if you thought it was the right thing. Obviously, you think it is."

"You can see as well as I can that he's not getting better. If anything, he's looking a lot worse."

Mom nodded. "He's definitely looked better."

"If I ever thought—"

"You don't have to explain. I understand." Mom checked her watch. "I should probably see about catching a meeting."

So much for the idea of keeping Mom's stress in check.

4

"WHEN DID YOU DECIDE?" VERONICA asked me a few minutes after Mom left for AA.

"A couple days ago."

She nodded. "That's what I thought."

"You did?"

"Yeah. You've been acting differently."

"No, I haven't."

"You have definitely not been your flirty self."

I wasn't even sure that was possible. "Sure I have," I said.

"No, you haven't."

"Maybe I just finally figured what was the point?"

"Good conversation and easy banter are always fun."

"Yeah. I guess I just ran out." I looked her in the eye. "Tell me, how many times have you had a family member pull the plug on one of your patients?"

"A little more than half the time."

"So, I'm not alone in this."

"Far from."

"Do you think I'm making the right call?"

"That's not for me to say."

"Come on. You're the professional. You've got to have an opinion."

"Not one I'm willing to share."

"Why not? You've been here as long as me. You've seen everything that I have."

"Because it's not my place to give it."

I couldn't believe this. "You really won't tell me if you think I'm doing the right thing or not?"

"If I disagree with you, you'll dismiss my opinion and find someone else who does agree with you. But if I do agree with you, you'll use it to justify your decision. And if at some point in the future you regret turning the machines off, you'll blame me, because you'll say my opinion is what cemented your decision."

"No, I wouldn't."

"That's not a risk I'm willing to take."

Of all the people I thought I could rely on, Veronica had turned out to be no better than the others.

"Well then, thanks for nothing," I said, and turned my back on her as I headed back to the kitchen.

"Danny...you know there's reasons behind all the rules I have."

Her words stopped me. *Yeah.* The same was true with the rules I lived by too.

Without turning around, I asked, "Lessons learned the hard way?"

After a few seconds, Veronica answered, "This one was

learned the hardest way."

I slowly turned around to face her. Whatever memory our conversation had dredged up still evidently pained her.

"All right," I said. "I won't try to put you in a position to break it."

"Thank you." A touch of a smile returned to her lips.

"But I do know a couple other positions that would be fun if your other rule does ever crack," I said, and gave her a wink.

"Here we go again," she said with an exaggerated eye roll.

"Hey, you're the one who said you missed my flirting."

5

"BILLY'S TRUST IS COMPLETELY BULLETPROOF."

That's what Martin Havenhurst, attorney at law, told me from behind the oversized mahogany desk that probably overcompensated for the same thing the sports car I was sure was parked down on the street twelve stories below.

I put Havenhurst in his mid-forties, maybe early fifties. He was the attorney who'd put Billy's trust together. Since he'd written the thing up, he seemed like the best person to defend it in court against my nutball sister. I'd given him a call, and he told me to come meet him at his office in Riverside the next morning.

"You sure about that?" I asked.

"Absolutely. And since everything Billy owns goes to his son when the boy turns twenty-one, your sister can't claim there's a monetary motive for your compliance with the medical directive. Her complaint completely lacks merit."

I wasn't so sure about that. "Have you read the crap that she's saying?"

"Oh, yes. She does an excellent job of making you out to be a real douchebag."

"I can't say your agreeing with her is instilling much confidence in me."

"Relax, Dan. All lawyers make the opposition seem like douchebags. It's what we're paid to do. It's what you want me to do to her, isn't it?"

Put that way, I could only agree with him. "I just want this bullshit to go away," I said.

"And it will. Christina Meacham has an incredible reputation as a prosecutor. When my wife goes up against her, she advises her clients to take the plea bargain. But this isn't a criminal matter. Your sister's swimming in my part of the ocean now. What she alleges, even if true, is not enough for a judge to undo the medical directive."

"You're positive about that?"

"Yes. You've got nothing to be afraid of."

"I didn't say I'm afraid of her," I said, probably too defensively.

"I was referring to the weight of her complaint," Havenhurst said. "Now, have you or anyone else seen Billy move or show any signs of life these last five weeks?"

"If we had, I wouldn't even be considering pulling the plug."

"Right. And since no one has seen anything that can be considered a legitimate sign of life out of him this entire time, the court will be inclined to listen to the doctor."

"In other words, you're going to kick her ass."

"Up the block and around the corner."

"Then I must've come to the right place."

"Without a doubt."

I stood and approached his desk. Havenhurst rose as well. We shook hands.

"We'll need to meet up again to go over your testimony," he said, "but other than that, this should be one short and quick court appearance."

"All right. Sounds good."

"You have any more questions for me?"

"Yeah, I'm just curious. How did Billy find you for putting his trust together?"

"Oh, well, my wife was with the public defender's office and had represented him in a couple DUIs. He called her to see about a trust, and she referred him to me."

"Ah, that makes sense."

"Only time it's ever happened. Usually the people she represents don't wind up with the need for a trust."

He walked me to his office door and opened it.

I asked, "When you wrote up Billy's trust, did he ever tell you why he wanted to name me as his agent and all that?"

"I don't recall discussing it much with him. He did say you'd be the right guy for the job."

How the hell had Billy come to that conclusion? *Must've been the drugs.*

"Did he happen to tell you that we don't speak to each other?" I asked.

Havenhurst raised his eyebrows. "He said you were fine with it. I have all of my clients talk to the people they name before we finalize the document."

"Can't say that ever happened."

"Are you screwing with me?"

"Looks like Billy screwed with us both."

6

I GOT BACK TO BILLY'S house about twenty minutes after twelve. The custody change had already taken place and Mom had left. I found Dad in the living room with Veronica once again doing his worst to get her to compromise her standards.

"So, what's your favorite type of food?" he asked her.

"Oh, that's easy. Italian."

"You don't say. You know, I know this little hole-in-the-wall place in Corona that has the best veal parmigiana. We should go there one of these nights."

"Dad," I said, interrupting his attempt. "Veronica's running a marathon next weekend. She can't be loading up on food like that."

Dad looked like he wanted to punch me. I looked past him and winked at Veronica.

"So how'd things go with Billy's lawyer?" she asked.

"Tina doesn't have a leg to stand on."

I went into the kitchen and got a Diet Dr. Pepper from the fridge. As I closed the door, I found Dad standing there with a perplexed look on his face.

"What?" I asked.

"I think I know a way to settle this thing between you and Tina."

"There's nothing to settle. Billy's wishes are clear, and Tina's wrong."

"You're probably right, but I've also lived long enough to know that even when things seem clear, you never know what might happen in court."

My suspicion level immediately went up to ten. Dad wouldn't have said that for no reason at all.

"What are you getting at, Dad?"

"Just hear me out. I know you need to get back to Vegas, and Tina—"

"This has nothing to do with me going back to Vegas."

"But you do need to go back, don't you?"

"Yeah, but—"

"So why not go back now? I'll stay here and take care of Billy, and I'm sure Tina will drop her case. It's a win-win-win for everybody."

"Especially for you, huh? Get you out of that one room you're renting. wouldn't it?"

"I offered to take care of Billy from the start."

"I said no then, and I'm saying no now."

"You're really that committed to pulling the plug on him?"

"I'm doing what he said he wants. Read his trust."

"I know, but what if he only needs another month or so?"

"Or maybe another year or two? He's not getting better. Even if he was, I'd still never leave the Prick in your care."

I couldn't believe the words had come out. But they had. Dad had pushed me too far.

For the first time in a long time, I saw him get mad. Really mad.

"I know you resent me for not always being around when you were growing up, but I was doing my damnedest to provide for my family."

"Oh, cut the crap. Mom worked a lot more than you, and she was always there. For all of us."

"You always take her side. You are aware she's the one who divorced me and took my house, right?"

"It wasn't your house. It was our house, which you were seldom at. And Mom's only mistake was not divorcing you years before."

Dad looked down. When he lifted his head, I saw his eyes were red. The anger was gone. He seemed to be on the verge of tears.

"All right. I'll admit that maybe I wasn't the best father…"

I couldn't argue with that. Nor would I console him.

"Danny, I'm begging you here. Please… let me help."

"I don't need your help, Dad. Neither does Billy. And this conversation is over."

"Just—"

"Just nothing. You can either shut up or you can get

the hell out."

Dad opted to keep his mouth closed, but I could tell he didn't want to. He left in a huff. And while I should've been more than happy to have an entire afternoon alone with Veronica, I kept wondering what conspiracy against me Tina and Dad had concocted.

That got me stuck in an anxious worry loop until the next morning, when I found out what the two had come up with to stop me from carrying out Billy's wishes.

7

My phone rang at nine twenty-seven a.m. This instantly made me tense. Mom was here, so it wasn't her. Maybe it was Big Paul. No, it was too early. I saw a 951 area code on the screen but didn't recognize the number. I picked it up. It was Martin Havenhurst. I thought he was calling to discuss preparations for my upcoming court testimony.

Nope.

"Dan, I think we might have encountered a complication," Havenhurst said after we exchanged the required hellos.

"What kind of a complication?" I asked.

"The kind that we don't want to be dealing with in court tomorrow. I just emailed you a document. It's a sworn affidavit from your father that your sister's filed. Give it a read and call me back at this number."

Before I could object, Havenhurst hung up. Whatever this affidavit was, I didn't want to read it. But I knew I had to.

I went to the email app on my phone and found

Havenhurst's message. I opened the PDF and quickly read it. It was a statement by Dad with a bunch of legal mumbo jumbo at the top, but the body of it was quite clear.

I, James Meacham, am the father of William Meacham. Since March 4, 2017, William has been in a coma following a car accident. He was first cared for at Loma Linda Hospital. He was then transported to his residence in Norco, where he has been in the care of my older son, Daniel Meacham. Daniel has been caring for William, with the assistance of a visiting nurse, since March 13, 2017.

In the last week, on multiple occasions, I have witnessed William's eyelids twitch.

What the hell?

I looked over at Billy. His eyelids hadn't twitched. Not once.

On April 1, 2017, I witnessed William's right index finger move. I am uncertain who else might have seen these or other movements by William. I told my son Daniel about the movements I observed. He showed no interest in hearing about this, became angry, and told me I should "get the hell out."

What bullshit!

That wasn't what happened. This didn't even sound like Dad.

I redialed Havenhurst and told him that as soon as he

got on the line.

"That's the biggest April Fools' prank I've ever seen," I nearly screamed. "Billy hasn't moved at all."

"Your father says he has."

"He's lying."

"That's a very serious accusation."

"His name may be on it. But those are my sister's words."

"Then are you saying that she's seen your brother move?"

"The last movement Billy made was headlong into a telephone pole!"

"And you're positive about this? There hasn't even been any type of twitch?"

"The only movements being made by Billy are farts, and that's because I'm feeding him."

"Okay," Havenhurst said. "We can handle this."

"You didn't sound so confident when you called."

"I needed to know that you had been on the up and up with me."

"What? Do you think I'm trying to kill my brother too?"

"Calm down. I didn't say that. I just needed to make sure I had the complete story from you. The court will take seriously any credible witness saying they saw movement by your brother."

"My dad is far from a credible witness."

"To you, maybe, but you're not the court."

"Tina put him up to this. He's not smart enough to have come up to this on his own."

"Regardless, unless I can get him twisted up during cross and you can help me impeach him, the court might be sympathetic to your sister's complaint."

"In other words, I could get screwed."

"Not entirely. I assume there are other people who have been with Billy regularly who can contradict your father's affidavit."

I looked over at Mom and Veronica, who silently watched me as I spoke to Havenhurst.

"Yeah," I said. "My mom and Billy's nurse."

"That's perfect. Your mother should be able to cancel out your dad, and the nurse will give us professional, third-party credibility. We won't need them to testify at the hearing, but if you can get them to each write out an affidavit about what they've witnessed with Billy, that will go a long way in bolstering your testimony and discrediting your father's."

"Okay. I can do that."

"Good. Now, the judge might grant the injunction against you terminating life support, but even if that were to happen, it's doubtful you'd be removed as Billy's agent."

"I thought you said the trust is bulletproof."

"It is, but I just want you to be prepared for all possible contingencies."

"Like I said. I could get screwed."

8

"ALL YOU HAVE TO DO is write out what you've seen and what you haven't when you've been by Billy's side."

"I don't think I can," Mom said without any hesitation.

It took all of my strength to hold my anger in check. I'd used Billy's computer to print the affidavit forms Martin Havenhurst had sent me. I wasn't sure why Billy even had a printer, as I figured this was the only time Word had even been opened and used on the damn thing. I definitely didn't want to open his web browser and examine the history there.

I'd thought Veronica might have some reservations about writing out an affidavit, given her rule. She didn't. Without any hesitation, she'd taken the form from me and gone into the kitchen to write out what she'd observed while caring for Billy the last month.

It was Mom who presented the problem.

"Why can't you?" I asked her.

"This is between you and your sister."

"No. This is about Billy and what's in his trust."

"I don't know what you'd want me to write."

"Only the truth. That you haven't seen Billy move."

Mom didn't answer.

"Have you?" Maybe she had and the Prick only refused to move around me. I could see him doing that. Mom, though, shook her head.

"Okay, I said, "then there's no reason not to write that down."

"But what if your father did?" Mom asked.

"Really? After all these years, *now* you're going to start believing what Dad says?"

"Of course not, but with something like this... I'd like to."

Mom looked at the carpet. This whole situation was taking a bigger toll on her than I'd realized. At least she was being honest with me. I just had to get past her heart to reach her head in this matter.

"I wish he had moved too," I said, not knowing if that were true. "But he hasn't. You know that."

Mom nodded.

"Then you'll write an affidavit?"

She shook her head. "I can't."

"Mom!"

"What if I'm wrong?"

"What's wrong with saying what you haven't seen?"

Mom didn't reply.

"Fine. Then Tina's going to win, Dad will become Billy's caregiver, and my ass is going back to Vegas. But at least Billy won't be in a home. And since I'll be out of here, you can let Jessie and her little bastard come visit as much as they want."

Moving faster than I thought she could, Mom swung her left hand and caught me with an open palm across my face. It stunned me. I couldn't recall the last time she'd slapped me. I stared at her, not sure what to say. It didn't matter. Mom was pissed and did all the talking.

"I know and understand how you feel about Jessie. But you will not talk like that about my grandson ever again."

I knew I should say something, but had no idea what. Mom grabbed her purse and gripped her oxygen device as she turned for the door.

"Mom—"

"I'm going to a meeting," Mom said without looking back.

She slammed the door when she left.

Great.

I'd managed to alienate the last family member still somewhat on my side.

I turned around and saw Veronica standing there, holding her affidavit.

Yeah, just great.

9

I SAT AT THE DINING room table trying to figure out what I should do next when Veronica intruded upon my thoughts.

"If you drank, I'd offer to go get you a bottle of your favorite," Veronica said as she slowly approached me.

I gave her the best smile I could muster. "There's a part of me that thinks today might be as good a day as any to start."

"Things like this are extremely hard on a family."

"Especially one as screwed up as this one."

"Your family members have a pretty large number of idiosyncrasies, but how they're all acting in this situation isn't that unique."

"No?" I asked, finding her statement nearly impossible to believe.

"No," she said, and sat in the chair beside me. "Mine pretty much acted the same way."

I looked at Veronica intently. She wasn't talking to me as Billy's nurse at that moment. Her words were coming from somewhere else. I briefly considered asking something that would prompt her to elaborate but felt remaining silent would be a better course of action.

It was. Taking a deep breath, Veronica continued.

"About five years ago… No, actually, it's been more than six now. Six years ago, my grandfather had a massive heart attack. They needed to do a quadruple bypass if he was going to stay alive. During the surgery, he went into a cardiac arrest. The surgeons were able to revive him, but he never came to after. His brain had been deprived of oxygen for a pretty long time. He never woke up."

"So, he was brain dead?"

"That's the way it looked to me," she said. Veronica looked away. "And when my mom asked me what I thought about his chances of recovering, I told her that didn't seem likely. She told her brothers and sisters, and they told my grandmother that. And based on my professional opinion, she asked the hospital to discontinue life support. Three days later, my grandfather was dead."

I sat beside Veronica silently. She still didn't look me in the eye, which was slightly odd. During the past month, she'd never been shy about locking pupils with me. Yet I could see in her face the emotional pain she still felt from this memory. I wasn't sure if I should say something or not. While trying to figure that out, Veronica spoke again.

"I never doubted the decision. I knew he was gone. My mom's youngest sister wasn't so convinced. She got most of my cousins spun up about it, saying my mom and I were just after Grandpa's money—which made no sense, as what little he did have was going to my grandma—but it stuck. By the time his funeral came around, even my grandmother was questioning the decision. Then a little more than a year later, she died of what everyone says was a broken heart."

Veronica finally looked at me. Her eyes were wet, but she used all of her inner strength to prevent the tears from falling.

"Needless to say," she said, "my mom and I haven't been included in any family holidays or parties since then."

Veronica wiped her eyes and sat taller in the chair. She met my eyes and said, "And now you know how I came up with that rule."

We sat at the table looking at each other, not saying a word for almost a minute.

Finally, I leaned closer to her and said, "If we hadn't thrown out all of Billy's booze, I'd offer you a drink."

"Well, I've got my race coming up, so I couldn't drink it even though I'd like to."

She didn't move back. I continued to bring my face closer to hers.

"I might know a way or two that we could console each other."

"Oh, really?"

"Uh-huh."

My lips were near hers. In another few seconds we'd be kissing. In another few minutes we'd be ripping each other's clothes off.

Or so I thought.

Veronica stood up before my lips could reach hers.

"That was very smooth," she said. "But I didn't tell you all that to invite you to make a move on me. I told it to you so that you'd know you weren't alone in what you're dealing with."

"Right."

Veronica turned away from me and returned to the living room with Billy.

I thought I'd finally been in the position to close the deal with Veronica, but I'd misread the situation.

Dammit. Dammit! DAMMIT!

10

WITH DAD SQUARELY ON TINA'S side and Mom not willing to put herself in the middle of it, I had no choice but to turn to God.

Well, maybe not God exactly—more like the only preacher I was on speaking terms with. I'd called Sergio and asked him to come over. He said he'd be by in the evening. The stress had gotten to me. I needed to unwind, so I went out to the hot tub to try to unkink the knots in my neck and back.

As the warm water and the jet-driven bubbles worked me over, I rested my head back on the concrete behind the hot tub.

"I shoulda brought my trunks," I heard Sergio say.

I opened my eyes and looked straight up to find him standing over me.

"I'm just in my chonies," I told him. "Feel free to do the same. As long as they're clean."

"What makes you think I'm wearing any?" he said with a smirk.

"That sounds kinda scandalous for a Bible thumper."

I pushed myself off the step I sat on and moved across the bubbling tub so I could look across at Sergio. He sat on the edge of the tub after I moved, taking off his shoes.

"Have I thumped you with my Bible once since you've been here?"

"Just an expression," I said. "No offense."

"None taken."

Sergio now had his shoes and socks off. He rolled up his pant legs and dipped his feet into the steaming white water.

"How's everything going?" he asked.

"Honestly? Pretty shitty."

"What you've been asked to do would be hard, no matter what."

"Believe it or not, Billy's not the biggest pain in my ass right now. It's Tina."

"She always liked to be in control of everything as long as I've known you. Her not trying to control the situation would have been a bigger surprise."

"I'm trying to see that Billy's wishes are followed through, and she's suing to stop me."

"That might explain why I hadn't heard from her in the last few days."

I screwed up my courage and went for the next part. "I know I probably don't have any room to ask you for a favor, but you may be the only person left that can talk her down from this."

"I'm not sure what I could say to her."

"Why? You agree with her? If I pull the plug, it's going to give Billy an express ticket to the great Satanic barbecue?"

"Is that what Tina told you?"

"Yeah. If I pull the plug, she says I'll be sending Billy straight to hell."

"Let me assure you: whatever happens, Billy's not going to hell."

"Oh, you're telling me after all the crap he's done that he doesn't belong there?"

"We all belong there, Danny. Even me. But thankfully, God's grace is greater than all of our sin combined."

"That's right. Ask Jesus for forgiveness and all is good. Is that how it works? Is that what Billy did? Is that how he slipped out of getting his?"

"You were gone a pretty long time. There's a lot you don't know."

"Exactly. That's the way I wanted it. That's how I'd like to keep it."

"I can sympathize with that, but you asked me about Billy going to hell, so let me tell you what I do know. After he hit the Lotto, he really wanted a new life. Billy tried damn hard to get it together and stay clean. He gave his life to God. He made a big effort. I really thought he was going to make it. But then they prescribed him those pills for his back pain, and that pulled him back under deeper than he'd been before."

"Sounds just like Billy."

"But he still gave his heart to Jesus. Despite everything he's done, his sins are forgiven. While he may appear guilty to us in the natural, he's innocent in the eyes of God. And when he dies—whenever or however that may happen—Billy will go into the presence of God, not anywhere else."

I thought it over and shook my head. "You know what? That's bullshit."

"It's the Gospel," Sergio said.

Those words made me snap. I stood up in the hot tub, pointing my finger at Sergio.

"Your gospel. Not mine. You know as well as I do that that asshole is far from innocent. God can forgive him all he wants. I won't."

"Danny... I'm sorry."

As soon as he said that, the anger that had been simmering in me came bubbling out.

"You know what the two most useless words in the English language are?" I asked Sergio as I glared at him. "*I'm sorry*. That's what everyone says when they hurt you and pretend they didn't mean to. *I'm sorry*. That's what Billy said every time he screwed me over. *I'm sorry*. It's what Jessie said when I found out about them. *I'm sorry*. It's like people believe that stupid, little meaningless phrase will just make everything better. It doesn't."

Sergio was about to respond, but I didn't want to hear it.

I climbed out of the hot tub, went to the edge of the pool, and dove in. The water was cold, especially after my

227

time in the Jacuzzi, but it didn't matter. I went to the bottom and stayed there as long as I could. When I came up for air, Sergio had left.

What a lucky son of a bitch. He could leave here whenever he wanted. They all could. Everyone could except me. Except me and Billy. I was tethered to that asshole lying in a coma in the living room.

11

COURT WAS ONLY A DAY away and things weren't looking as bulletproof to me as they had when I first went to Havenhurst's office. That meant I had no choice but to take a run at Dad myself that next morning.

After he and Mom separated, Dad had started renting a room from Charlie Purkiss over on River Road. Dad had moved there after losing the house to Mom in the divorce. Charlie was between wives and had a room to rent. I went up to the front door and rang the bell. No answer. I knocked. Still nothing.

Dad's Corvette was in the driveway. He was there but hiding from me. Tina had probably told him to do that if I came around. I had to try something.

"Dad, I know you're here. Just come to the door so we can talk."

He responded with the silence I'd become accustomed to from Billy. He could hear me. I knew it. I went for trickery to get his attention.

"Veronica's been asking about you. If you want to come by and see her and Billy, I can take off for a while.

Just let me know."

Even offering Veronica up as a sacrifice, I couldn't get an answer from Dad.

"Fine, then. I'll see you in court. We both know you're lying, and you're gonna regret signing that affidavit. I promise you."

I got in the Supra and headed back for the house. I was hungry and hadn't eaten anything before leaving. I thought about stopping by Pat's Kitchen for an early dinner, but I didn't want to run the risk of running into anyone. Instead, I turned into the Circle K. I could get some munchies there.

Climbing out of the Supra, I looked out at Sixth Street and the passing traffic. It was on the street out front of the store that Billy had crashed my Nissan. He'd asked me to borrow it so he could come here to buy some dip. I refused. First, I didn't want him driving my car. Second, he didn't have a license.

That didn't stop him.

While I was practicing in my room, he took my keys and drove off with my car. There wasn't a stoplight at Center and he foolishly crossed the four lanes of Sixth in busy afternoon traffic, getting t-boned and rolling my car. He walked away with a cut on his forehead, but my Nissan was totaled.

I'd wanted to press charges, but the cop who responded to the accident didn't seem interested. I wanted to make my case that Billy should be arrested for stealing my car, but Mom pulled me away from that. She told me what Billy had done had been wrong, but I should be grateful he'd walked away from the crash.

I wasn't. If the Prick was going to steal and wreck my car, he could have done me the favor of dying too.

That memory gave me the chills. I'd wished him dead back then.

Am I working as hard as I am to turn off Billy's life support now to make up for him surviving eighteen years ago?

No. That wasn't why. It was the right thing to do.

If I were flat on my back in a coma wasting away like he was, I wouldn't consider it living either. I'd want whoever might be in charge to let me die. And I was sure Tina would have tried to keep me alive as a vegetable anyway.

That damn Tina.

I went into the convenience store, grabbed a pack of powdered Donettes, and filled up a forty-four-ouncer of Diet Dr. Pepper. I put them both on the counter and looked at the clerk. It was the buxom tattooed young woman who'd been skinny-dipping in Billy's pool with Eric Parker and Bald Tommy. Her last words about me being a real asshole reverberated in my ears as I looked at her.

We did each other the courtesy of not greeting or speaking to each other in any way. Her nametag revealed her name to be Kaitlyn. As she rang up the order, I noticed a framed picture hanging behind her.

The photo was of Billy posing with a thin, balding man in a suit, and a cute girl in a Circle K uniform. I didn't realize the girl was Kaitlyn at first as her arms lacked the tattoos she'd obviously gotten since that day.

Billy stood between her and the balding man holding an oversized cardboard check. The Prick had the biggest shit-eating grin on his face that I'd ever seen. And why shouldn't he have? He'd just hit the Lotto for $27 million.

"You sold him that ticket?" I asked Kaitlyn.

"Yep. Only big winner we ever had," she said.

"You should've made him cut you in for a percentage."

"He did buy me that car." Kaitlyn pointed out the front window to the Ford Escort parked in front of the store that had seen its better days.

"Hmm."

"How's Billy doing?" she asked.

"Not any better than the night you saw him."

Kaitlyn nodded sadly. I handed her the cash for my purchase. She silently gave me my change, and I turned for the doors.

But before I could take a step toward them, I froze. Standing there, looking up at me, was the Kid.

12

"YOU'RE MY UNCLE DANNY, AREN'T you?" the Kid asked.

"Can't say that I am." I pushed past him for the doors.

"You're not Danny Meacham?" he asked from behind.

I turned to face the Kid, putting my back to the glass door to push through since both of my hands were full.

"Yeah. But I'm not your uncle."

I went outside and headed from the car. The Kid must've decided to follow me, as I heard his annoying preteen voice again.

"But you're my dad's brother. That makes you my uncle, doesn't it?"

"Not this time," I told him, and set the Donettes on the roof of the Supra so I could fetch the key from my pocket.

"Why are you driving my dad's car?" he asked like I was a thief or something.

I felt ashamed initially then got over it. Who was this kid to badger me?

"Shouldn't you be in school?" I asked.

"I get out at 2:30."

Of course he did. I clicked the door open and turned my back on the Kid, but he wasn't letting up.

"Can I ask you something?" he said.

"You just did." I grabbed the Donettes off the roof.

"How come I can't come and see my dad?"

"'Cause it's not a good idea."

Before I could get into the car, he sprung another question on me.

"He's not going to wake up, is he?"

That stopped me. I knew the truth. I was fighting my sister in court because she wouldn't accept it. The Kid apparently understood what Tina's overeducated ass didn't. And I didn't want him to know he was right. But if he wasn't right, then that meant I was wrong.

"It's not looking good," I admitted without looking at him.

"I'd really like to see him before he dies," he said, and that was just enough to push me too far.

"He's a drug addict and a complete fuck-up. Why do you even care about him?"

Dammit. Why'd I say that?

I looked at the Kid. Tears welled up in his eyes.

"Because he's my dad, asshole."

Being shorter than me, the Kid had a better angle on his target. There was no way I could block him as he swung his fist up and punched me in the balls.

I hadn't been racked in the nuts in years. The pain shot

out to every other part of my body as I doubled over, dropped the Donettes, and spilled my soda down the front of my pants.

When I looked up, the Kid had already run to his bike. He was on it now and pedaling away as fast as his legs could go. I wanted to call after him, but after years of forcing the boy's existence out of my mind, I couldn't remember his name.

"Hey! Wait!" I yelled in a higher-pitched voice than I usually had.

The Kid looked back at me. His cheeks were wet with tears, but the hurt and sadness in his eyes was gone. It'd been replaced by anger and rage. I'd seen that look, that rage, many times before. I'd seen it in Billy's eyes every time he was pissed at me. I now saw it in the Kid's eyes.

The Kid flipped me off as he pedaled around the corner and up Center Street towards where I knew Jessie's mom's house was.

What the hell was wrong with me?

13

"WE HAVE A LITTLE ACCIDENT?" Veronica said as soon as I stepped into the Prick's house. She didn't even try to suppress her amusement at my appearance.

I ignored her and headed for the stairs. Her comment, though, had drawn Mom's attention.

"What happened?" Mom asked, coming my way with her oxygen machine and staring at my wet pants.

"Nothing," I lied.

"Your lap's telling a different story."

"Not now, Mom."

"Danny, putting off talking about whatever is bothering you isn't going to make anything better."

"Nothing's going to make anything better. Haven't you figured that out yet?"

"I don't understand," Mom said.

"Neither do I. I don't understand why Billy made me his agent. I don't understand why I came home. And I don't understand why I'm fighting with Tina over what happens to him."

"Because you're following your brother's wishes."

"My brother." The term burned like acid on my tongue. "That prick stopped being my brother a long time ago."

"Do not call him that word."

"Go ahead, slap me if you want, but you know it's true. It's what he is. Why else do you think he put me in this spot? Because he's a grade-A, world-class prick."

"That's not true!"

"Oh yeah, it is. I'm just the only one in this insane family who's got the guts to say it out loud."

"That's not why he chose you!"

"Oh yeah? You have another explanation? Do you?"

"He chose you because I did!"

Mom's words brought silence to the house. I couldn't believe it.

"You mean...you mean *you* put him up to this?"

"Of course not."

"Then what did you mean?"

"I told Billy to get that trust. That way, if something bad happened to him, Mason would be taken care of."

"And you also told him to name me as his agent, huh?"

"No—"

"Bullshit. I know you told him to name me."

"It wasn't like that."

"Sure it wasn't."

"When he was working on it, he asked me who I gave the power-of-attorney to in my will."

It took a few seconds for what she said to filter into my

brain, but once it did, my anger went up.

"Wait. You mean you made me your agent too?"

"Who else could I trust to do the right thing in the worst circumstance? Billy wouldn't be able to deal with it. Tina would keep me alive until the Second Coming. And even if I could consider your father—which I never would—we both know that he couldn't be trusted with something like that."

"So, you laid it all on me and didn't even think it was something worth mentioning?"

"I probably should have, but I didn't want you to say no."

"And you told Billy all of this?"

"Danny… he wanted to name me."

I could see the anguish in Mom's eyes, but I didn't care anymore.

"So you steered him toward me instead," I said.

"You're not a parent. You don't understand. That isn't something I could handle doing for any of you."

"Instead, you punt it to me."

"Danny, I'm sorry."

That was it for me.

"Yeah. Me too. But you know what? He's not worth fighting over. I'm done."

"You're what?"

"I'm done. I'm out. I'm going back to Vegas. Tell Tina she wins."

I turned my attention to Veronica. Again, she'd

witnessed the whole thing. Not that it mattered anymore. She'd had a front-row seat to Family Dysfunction Theater for a month. None of this should've shocked her anymore.

"If you're ever up my way," I told Veronica, "you've got my number, and you won't be working for me, so let's grab dinner."

With that, I went to the front door. Whatever things I had upstairs, I didn't need to take with me.

Mom called after me, "Danny, you can't leave. You have to take care of Billy."

"Not anymore, Mom. I quit."

I grabbed the doorknob and was ready to walk out of Billy's house, leaving him, my clinically deranged family, and all the BS of the past behind me.

The past, however, had a different idea.

It was walking up the pathway from the driveway.

And the past was fuming.

14

"YOU CAN HATE ME ALL you want, but you will not be an ass to my son!"

I'd only seen Jessie mad a couple of times, but never like this. At a deep level, I knew what she yelled at me was right, but she was the last person who had any standing to yell at me for any reason.

"He started it!" I shouted back, not sure why that was my chosen response.

"He's eleven years old."

"Then he's old enough to know that no means no. Oh, but then again, you're not exactly the best person to teach him about that."

"This isn't about us. It's about what you said to Mason."

"Us? Us? Who are you to talk to me about us? I once thought there was an us, but you more than proved me wrong about that."

"We were on a break."

"So, you decided to use the opportunity to jump my brother."

"You left me, Danny."

"I went on tour with my band. It's what you do when you're trying to make it."

"And how'd that work out for you?"

Who the hell was she to say that to me?

I let the Slut have it.

"It would have worked out fine if you'd kept your legs closed."

"Oh, everything's all my fault."

"No. It's his!" I screamed, pointing back toward the Prick inside the house. "His whole life, he screwed me over. And when I wasn't around, he set his sights on you. And you were stupid enough to fall for his bullshit."

"The only bullshit I ever fell for was yours."

"I treated you like gold."

"Gold isn't the word I'd choose."

"Oh, I was such a bad boyfriend."

"You were hardly a boyfriend at all. You only had time for me after rehearsal or after you were done writing or after your gigs. When you wanted to see a movie, or especially when you wanted to get laid. Your music always came first. And if I was second, it was a distant one."

"Now it makes sense. Billy, the jobless wonder, didn't have any ambition, so he could just be there to meet all of your needs that I couldn't."

"As many problems as Billy's had, letting me know that he loved me was never one of them."

"Then you should have married him."

"If he could've stayed sober, I probably would have."

I pushed by her and went to my Mitsubishi parked on the side of the house. As I got in, I looked out at Jessie.

"Well, he's sober now," I said. "Hasn't had anything in a month. He's all yours. Till death do you part."

15

I CALLED BIG PAUL AS I sped down the hill of Hidden Valley Parkway on my way to the 15 freeway and freedom.

I needed to get back to Vegas. I needed to get on stage with my band. I needed to find a young, willing project who didn't want to talk much, or at all. I needed to get back into my normal life and normal routine. That would put the family I was cursed to be born into and the Slut out of my mind.

"Hey, Danny, how's your brother doing?" Paul asked upon answering.

"It doesn't look too good."

"Oh man, that's too bad."

"Yeah, well, he brought it on himself."

There was silence from Paul. He probably didn't know how to respond to that, which was okay. I had no desire to talk about Billy any longer than I had to.

"I'm on my way back," I said. "I'll probably need tonight to get settled in, but I should be able to make rehearsal tomorrow."

Again Big Paul responded with silence. This

immediately alerted me that something was wrong.

"Tomorrow's Wednesday, right?" I asked. "Aren't we rehearsing?"

Big Paul let out a wimpish sort of sound you wouldn't think could come from a man his size. "Yeah, we're rehearsing. It's just that... Dammit... I've been putting off calling you."

More silence. Had they screwed things up? Had they gotten fired and not told me?

"Paul, what's going on, man?"

"Danny, there's really no easy way to say this, but the band's been doing pretty good with Rusty on vocals, and, well... we took a vote. We didn't see the need to have two lead singers."

"What? I started this band. It's my band. You can't kick me out."

"Yeah, we know that... Umm... we started a new one."

"Paul, you've been with me for seven years now. I've always taken care of you."

"No, you have, and I appreciate it. But splitting the money four ways instead of five has been pretty good the last few weeks... and we all want to keep it this way."

"All right. Fine. We'll let Rusty go and be a quartet again."

"Danny, let's be honest. Rusty's going places. We're talking about cutting an album, maybe even taking a trip to Nashville."

"You think he's gonna take you with him? That's bullshit. I can tell you a lot more about Nashville than any of you know."

"I'm sorry, Danny. The decision's already been made."

"You're sorry? Oh, you're going to be sorry! I'm gonna make you pay for this. You'll be sitting on the sidewalk outside of Caesars playing for tips when I'm done with you."

Big Paul's response was simple. He hung up on me.

I hit redial. As soon as the call connected, I saw the red brake lights in front of me. I was speeding right up on the back end of a truck and didn't have time to stop.

"Shit!"

I yanked the steering wheel to the right and hit the brakes hard to avoid the crash. Half of that worked out. I barely missed hitting the back end of the truck, but went across the horse trail and head-on into the cinder block retaining wall.

16

I'D NEVER BEEN IN A car accident before. Not even a fender bender. Billy had had three that I knew of, probably more.

His last one had brought me back to Norco a month ago. Now my first one had prevented me from leaving. Unlike the Prick, I'd had my seatbelt on. Plus, the Mitsubishi had an airbag that deployed and knocked the hell out of me. Unlike Billy's last accident, I was able to walk away from my first.

My Outlander, however wasn't in shape to drive to Vegas, or even to the corner. The front end had been smashed all to hell. Radiator and other fluids ran all over the place. A police car, fire engine, and ambulance responded to the crash. The firemen made sure my wrecked ride wouldn't explode then left. The paramedics checked me out and insisted I go to the hospital. I refused as politely as I could. The deputy called a tow truck that came and put my Mitsubishi up on a flatbed.

The driver asked where I wanted it towed. Billy's wasn't an option. Under the current conditions, neither was Mom's. I asked if he had a body shop he'd recommend. He did, so I had him take the Outlander there, even though I had no idea how I'd pay for the repairs or if my ride was even repairable.

About an hour later, the only sign of the accident was some debris left on the horse trail, dark gashes in the brick wall, and me standing by my lonesome with a bruised and swelling face. I didn't have anywhere to go and didn't know who I could call.

Well, not exactly. There was one person I could call, so I did.

There was a Chick-fil-A across the street from where I'd crashed. I hadn't been in one before. I'd always gone through the drive-thru when I craved one of their chicken sandwiches. It was amazingly clean inside. None of the workers bothered me as I sat at a rear table without ordering anything. I'd never realized they played Christian music inside until that moment. That made sense for a place that was closed on Sundays.

The Christian songs were interesting. The music sounded good, and the singers had great voices, but the lyrics were lame and all about the same thing—Jesus. I guessed that was what made it Christian music.

Sergio came through the doors and saw me right away. I knew he'd come.

"Wow," he said, approaching the table. "You okay?"

"Yeah. I'll be fine."

"You should probably have a doctor check you out,"

he said as he looked my face over.

"Paramedics already did. Nothing's broken."

Sergio nodded. "You hungry?"

"Not really."

"Well, I am, so you get to sit and watch me eat."

I nodded. Sergio went up to the counter and ordered. A minute or so later, he returned to the table with a mini pylon they seemed to use instead of order numbers.

When Sergio sat down, I finally asked him something that had started bugging me since my run-in with the Slut.

"I need to ask you something, and I want you to answer me honestly."

"Don't think I've ever lied to you."

I nodded. I doubt Sergio ever had. And as much as I wanted to hear his answer now, it frightened me that what he might say would be the brutal truth.

"Did I make a mistake by leaving the band?" I asked.

Sergio looked down at the table. "Man, that was a long time ago."

"Yeah, but do you think I made a mistake?"

"If I'd been in your boots, I probably would've done the same thing," he said, still not looking at me.

"You say you've never lied to me, but that's twice you didn't answer."

He took a moment, then said, "You never should have quit on us."

Finally, the truth.

"Lonnie begged me to keep the band together," I said.

"Why didn't you?"

"I'd known you longer, which meant I knew that when you wanted things your way, that's how it was going to be. You decided you were going to go for it on your own, and there wouldn't be any stopping you."

He was right. I leaned back in the seat and reflected on the last twelve years. Every dream I'd had. Not a single one of them had come true. They'd all burned up, their ashes scattered to the winds.

"I really screwed everything up, didn't I?" I said more to myself than to Sergio.

"Things worked out."

"For you, maybe. What do I have to show for my life?"

"You're still playing."

"'Cause it's the only thing I know how to do. And now my band's fired me. I'm thirty-seven years old and I've wasted my whole life."

"Is that what you think?" Sergio asked.

"It's what I know."

Sergio stood up. "Come on."

I didn't like this. "I'm not going back to Billy's."

"We're not. There's something I want to show you."

I *really* didn't like this. "What about your food?" I asked, seeking to delay whatever it was Serg had in mind.

"I'll take it to go. Come on."

17

SERGIO HAD THE TEENAGE WORKER bag up his food then drove us into town down Hamner. When we got to Second Street, he pulled into the L-shaped strip mall parking lot across the street from In-N-Out Burger. A 7-Eleven held down the corner as it had for years. He parked at a spot in front of Slicks Pool Hall, the notorious congregating spot for everyone who failed to get away from Norco or do anything significant with their lives.

"I'm not in the mood for pool," I told him.

"Me neither," he said, pulling his sandwich from the bag.

"Well, you know I don't drink, so why are we here?"

"Wednesday's karaoke night."

"And I'm definitely not doing that."

"That's fine, but can you see who's in there?"

I looked through the window. The same overweight man with long hair who'd accosted me in Target was doing a version of "L.A. Woman" that made Dad's singing seem tolerable.

"Circ-Ass Varg-Ass."

"Not Omar. The DJ."

I took a harder look inside at the man standing with the karaoke unit talking to a woman who'd just handed him a slip of paper. I hadn't noticed him at first, probably because I wasn't expecting to see him in there, but that face was unmistakable.

"Shit… Lonnie?"

"Yep," Sergio said between bites of his sandwich.

Lonnie had remained in good shape, but his hair had retreated significantly from the front lines. I sat there watching for a while as Sergio ate his sandwich and fries. Omar finished his song and Lonnie took the opportunity to sing "Friends in Low Places."

"How long's he been doing this?" I asked.

"I'm not completely sure. About three years ago, I came in here with some guys I play softball with, and there he was belting out the Garth."

"Still is." Lonnie had always been a huge Garth Brooks fan.

"Yeah. He always loved Garth."

"He see you?" I asked.

"Yeah. He was pretty embarrassed about it. So I made an excuse to leave early and never came back. Until now."

"If this is your way of making me feel like I'm *not* a total loser, you've done a pretty crappy job."

Sergio balled up the takeout bag and threw it at my door. It bounced harmlessly in my lap.

"Dammit, Danny. What's it going to take for you to

stop throwing yourself this pity party you've been having for the last dozen years?"

"Fine. You're right. I should've kept the band together and took you both with me to Nashville."

"This has nothing to do with the band. It's about you. You think we got all the gigs we did because we were great? We were good, but not that good. As much as I didn't want to admit it, Nick Z was right. It was your voice, your guitar, your stage presence that made us. That's what people came to see. You, Danny Mack. You know that. The songs you were writing, they were as good as anything being played on the radio. And much better than the crap they're putting out now."

Sergio took a breath, and I looked out the side window silently, hoping he was done. He wasn't.

"You could've been really big, Danny. You should've been. But for whatever reason, you threw it all away and became a Vegas lounge singer. That's the real tragedy."

How dare he say that to me?

I exploded.

"Don't you judge me! You didn't go through what I did!"

"You're right. I probably went through worse."

"Oh yeah, your life looks like it's been so rough."

"Sonia miscarried twice, you selfish prick! Once in the twenty-fourth week."

My defenses dropped. I wasn't sure when the twenty-fourth week of a pregnancy was, but I knew it wasn't a good thing. Sergio had never spoken to me like that ever before. He was simmering. I'd hurt him and felt totally shitty because of it.

"I... I didn't know," I said.

"Of course you didn't," he said, bringing his anger down. "You've been so stuck wallowing in your own heartbreak that you never stopped to think other people might have their own. I'd happily trade my losses for yours."

18

When Sergio pulled into Billy's driveway, I saw that both Mom's and Veronica's cars were still there. I hadn't wanted to come back here, but I had nowhere else to go. I'd figured Mom's Lexus would be but was surprised that Tina's Audi wasn't around. More surprising was the sight of Veronica's 4Runner.

I opened the passenger door of the Accord but didn't get out. Sergio and I hadn't spoken since going off on each other in Slick's parking lot. I felt something needed to be said before he left.

"Serg," I said, but stopped for a moment, unsure of how to say it. "How did you and Sonia get over all that?"

"You don't, really," he said, looking out the windshield, not at me. "You become somewhat numb to it and believe that God has a plan, and it all makes sense even if you don't understand it."

"And you really believe that?"

"I'd be a pretty horrible pastor if I didn't."

"So everything happens for a reason, huh?"

"That's not what I said." Sergio turned to me. He

wasn't angry, but confident as he spoke. "We all have free will to make our own decisions, but God's hand is definitely involved in directing our lives."

"I can't say that I believe that," I said.

"I understand that. But you do need to find a way to get past what happened with Billy and Jess."

"You think that's possible?"

"No. I believe it's essential."

I thought about it for a moment and decided that if anyone deserved the truth, it was Sergio, my best and possibly only friend.

"I can't."

"You should probably figure out how to, or you're going to wind up even worse off than your brother."

19

"GUESS I'LL OWE YOU SOME overtime," I said to Veronica as I walked into the living room from the front door.

As soon as she saw my purple, swollen face, Veronica sprang to her feet.

"What the hell happened to you?"

"Got in a bar fight."

"I thought you didn't drink."

"Yeah, well, I ordered one, was about to take a swig, and then I caught a right cross from some big biker dude, which has given me another reason to avoid the bottle."

"Right," she said, clearly not buying my story. Veronica gently put her hands on my face, checked me out, and said, "Your nose doesn't seem to be broken."

"Paramedics said the same thing."

"Must've been some brawl if they called the paramedics."

"It was insane."

"And this must've been a really big biker, 'cause his fist seems to have smashed up your entire face."

"Yeah. He had hands about the size of a Mitsubishi's

airbag."

"You were in an accident?"

"Yeah, me and a brick wall. But don't worry, the wall's fine."

"Did you go to the hospital?"

"No. I'm okay."

"Probably, but you should still get yourself checked out."

"That a professional or a personal recommendation?"

"A bit of both."

"I'll see how I feel tomorrow."

"I hate to tell you this, but it's going to feel and look worse tomorrow."

"Thanks for not sugarcoating it."

"You seem to appreciate the direct approach."

"I do. Thanks. Where's my mom?"

She motioned toward the Kid's room with her head. "I told her to get some sleep. She was exhausted."

It made sense Mom would choose the Kid's room. The stairs would've been too much for her. "My sister been by?"

"Uh-uh."

"There's a shock."

"I don't think your mom ever called her. She said she knew you'd be back."

"If it wasn't for that wall, I guarantee you I'd back in Vegas by now."

"Interesting."

"What is?"

"I felt confident you'd come back too."

"And what would give you that idea?"

"Just that if you were gonna bolt, you would've done it the first week."

I nodded. That logic did add up.

Veronica grabbed her Kindle from the comfy chair, put it in her bag, and zipped it up.

"I might come in a little later tomorrow if you're good with that," she said as she put her duffel over her shoulder.

"That's fine."

"You should ice your face for the swelling."

"Yeah. Okay."

Veronica went to the door. Before she could open it, I turned and asked her a question, and I wasn't even sure where it came from.

"Did Jessie come in after I left?"

She turned back to face me. "For a little while. Yeah."

"What did you think of her?"

"I'm a bit biased based on what I know from you. She seemed nice but sad. She's quite beautiful. I can see what attracted you. You really loved her, didn't you?"

I faced the far wall. I didn't want to look at either Billy or Veronica. I didn't want to answer that question, but for some reason I did.

"Yeah," I said. "It just clicked from the moment I met her. We were so good together. When I was on the road, I missed her in a way I couldn't explain. I wanted to marry her. That's why I'd come home, to propose to her. I figured she could move to Nashville with me, we could live together and then get married after a while. Being away from her made me realize how special she was. She's the only person I'd ever thought about being with forever. But as the song says, forever ain't as long as it used to be."

"I don't think I know that one," Veronica said from right behind me. I hadn't heard her step away from the doorway and come over. I turned and looked her in the eye.

"It was a great song. Probably the best I ever wrote."

Veronica motioned with her head toward Dad's Fender propped up against the wall. "Care to play it for me?"

"I don't want to wake up my mom."

"Then keep the volume low."

"It's been a long time."

"I'd really like to hear it."

I've had women look at me in my life. Many of them with a lustful desire. But only a few of them ever did so with genuine care and interest in me. That was the way Veronica was looking at me. She wasn't here because of what she could get from me. She was here because of me. It relaxed me, and I felt comfortable. At the same time, it scared me. Her eye contact with me never broke, and a voice in the back of my head told me what she had said: *It will be okay.*

I picked up Dad's black Strat and strummed it a little. Of course it was in tune. I turned on the amp and kept it at one, which was unusual.

I closed my eyes, digging deep into the depths of my mind for the song. It was there. A second later, my fingers played the melody and the lyrics sprang out of my mouth.

20

"Nothin' attracts the girls like playin' in a band
Makes no sense to settle down and put a ring on any hand
Then my eyes locked with hers and she stole my beatin' heart
I knew she was my meant to be from the very, very start
I pledged to her my faithful love forever and for all time
Then I found her pregnant with a kid that wasn't mine

Forever ain't as long as it used to be
When she says she loves you it ain't no guarantee
Don't fool yourself about some ole meant to be
When you're gone, she'll be livin' wild and free
'Cause forever ain't as long as it used to be

My heart broke into a billion pieces on that Godforsaken day
I had no idea what would cause my true love to go an' stray
I had to know the truth about who she'd betrayed me with
It turned out to be my wicked brother with whom she'd had her
    tryst

Forever ain't as long as it used to be
When she says I love you, it ain't no guarantee

Don't fool yourself about some ole meant to be
When you're gone, she'll be livin' wild and free
'Cause forever ain't as long as it used to be."

I hadn't sung that song in years. Yet I knew the words and chords like I'd just written them down in my red notebook.

I put down the Strat and turned off the amp. I suddenly found myself exhausted. I wanted to go to bed and sleep for hours.

"Wow," Veronica said.

"Yeah. Wow."

I looked at Veronica. Now she knew almost all of it. I was glad to see there wasn't pity in her eyes, but rather empathy. She really did get me. For some reason, I decided to tell her the rest.

"I wrote it the week after I caught 'em."

"Oh. That's how you found out?"

"No, not in the actual act, but the result of it. Jessie was already starting to show when I got back, and that was that. I left town the next day and officially moved to Nashville. Two weeks later, I wrote this song. And it got me a lot of attention. Brad Paisley's producer heard me play it at the Bluebird one night and wanted to put it on his next album. It would've been a huge hit right on there with 'Ticks' and 'Letter to Me.'"

"Why'd he change his mind?"

"He didn't," I said, and looked at the carpet. "As much

as I wanted to, I couldn't let him have it."

"I don't understand."

"It's one thing to be the laughingstock of your hometown because your brother knocked up your girlfriend. It's another to let the whole world know you got played the fool."

This created the biggest awkward moment I'd experienced with Veronica. I didn't have any words left in me. I'd never told anyone that whole story, especially not a beautiful woman I'd been attempting to lay for a month.

"Thank you for sharing that with me," she said.

"I'm not sure why I did."

"Probably 'cause you needed to."

She studied me for a long moment. Her eyes were boring into my soul. I wasn't sure how to respond, so I looked down at the carpet again.

"I'm gonna head home," Veronica said. "You should get some sleep yourself."

"Yeah, you're right. I need to be fresh for that hearing in the morning."

21

THE LAST TIME I'D WORN a suit was back in 1998. My high school graduation.

It hadn't really made any sense to wear it, since the blue imitation silk gown I had to wear covered it. Except you couldn't get into Disneyland for Grad Night without it, so at least it got some use.

Nineteen years later I needed a suit for court and didn't see the need to buy one for a single use. Billy, however, had one hanging in his closet. Probably for the myriad of court appearances he'd made over the years. It fit me well. Only problem being that I didn't know how to tie a tie.

I guess Billy didn't either. When I grabbed his one tie from where it hung, it was already knotted. The loop was big enough to fit over my head, so I got it on that way.

With Veronica not coming by till later, I fed Billy his breakfast. As his stomach directly consumed the nutrients being injected into it, I asked him. "You're sure you want me to do this? All you have to do is say stop, and I will."

He didn't respond.

"Okay. Just remember, this is what you wanted."

I then went into the Kid's room. Mom turned to face the door when I slowly opened it. I hadn't wanted to startle her awake, but it didn't matter. She'd been lying there in the bed under the *Star Wars* sheets already.

"Danny…" she said.

"Hey, Mom."

A look of horror entered her eyes when she saw me. "What happened to your face?"

"I tripped and fell down the stairs in the middle of the night."

"You could have really hurt yourself."

"It's a joke. It looks worse than it feels." That was a lie, but Mom didn't need anything else weighing on her.

She looked at me hard, then asked, "But are you okay?"

"I really can't say," I said, knowing she wasn't asking about my face this time.

"It's okay. I don't think any of us are."

"Of course not. We're the Meachams, remember?"

"I should've gone back to my maiden name. But I always hated being Carol Koskie. At least I got one good thing from your father."

"That's true."

"Actually, it was more than one."

I sat on the edge of the bed. We looked at each other. Relief filled Mom's eyes.

"If you're wearing that, then I suppose you're going to court."

"Yeah," I said. "How do I look? I mean, besides my busted-up face."

"Besides that, very handsome. Billy always wore that suit whenever he went to court."

"I kinda figured."

"He said it was his lucky suit."

"Did it bring him much luck?"

"He was usually guilty, so no. But they never sent him to jail, either."

"Well, hopefully, that'll be all the luck we need.

I kissed Mom on the cheek. That hurt my swollen lips, but I didn't mention it as I headed on my way for the legal face-off with my sister.

22

THE HEARING WAS HELD IN the Historic Courthouse in downtown Riverside and started promptly at nine a.m. Judge Jacobson, a woman in her fifties wearing heavy bifocals, monitored us from her perch on the bench. Tina sat at the table to the left of where I sat with Martin Havenhurst. Neither she nor I acknowledged each other. She didn't even ask me why I looked like I'd gone five seconds with Floyd Mayweather.

Tina's first witness was Dr. Pettis. She'd subpoenaed her too. The doctor seemed a strong witness for my position. Still, Tina managed to ask enough questions and raise enough doubt that even I wasn't sure if following Billy's wishes were the right thing to do.

The judge, however, wasn't convinced.

"Counselor," she said to Tina, "the doctor's testimony indicates to me that the medical requirements have been met to authorize the termination of life support. This is all in accordance with Mr. Meacham's medical directive."

"Normally, I'd concur, your honor," Tina said, "but I have a witness who can testify that there is significant brain activity to support the requested injunction."

"Objection, your honor," Havenhurst said. "Petitioner's witness is not qualified to give any testimony on Mr. Meacham's brain activity."

Tina immediately said, "The witness saw movement by the patient, which the respondent denies."

Havenhurst replied, "And the respondent has reason to believe this witness has been coached by opposing counsel in both his affidavit and the testimony he would provide the court."

Tina put on the hurt and offended act. "I have done nothing more than assist the witness in preparation for his testimony, which I'm sure Mr. Havenhurst knows is common in nearly every trial."

"But this isn't a normal witness," Havenhurst said. "This is the petitioner's father—"

"And the father of the patient—" Tina interrupted.

"And of my client, the respondent—"

Judge Jacobson cut them both off. "Which I gathered by reading the briefs filed by both of you. I'm going to allow the witness."

Tina smirked as she passed me on her way out to the hallway. Dad must be out there somewhere. I hadn't seen him earlier. She'd probably told him not to be around in case I tried to talk with him.

It was all on the line now. I'd soon know if Martin Havenhurst was worth the money I was paying him out of Billy's trust. If we lost, would Tina demand I pay the money back? Probably. She wasn't one to be content with winning. She liked to stomp the victory into you.

I put those thoughts out of my head as Dad came in. He too had decided to suit up, but I didn't know how much it mattered. His body bulged in the middle and the coat looked quite shabby. He'd probably had that thing in storage since the '84 L.A. Olympics. On top of that, he really needed to redo his dye job.

After the bailiff swore him in, Dad climbed into the witness box. Tina stood up. She seemed quite confident, compared to Dad, who fidgeted.

"Before you begin, counselor," the judge said, "I'm not new to matters such as these. If I sense anything unusual with this testimony, I will be very much open to jailing both you and the witness for contempt of this court."

"Of course, your honor," Tina said as she approached the witness stand.

I could see Tina's professionalism clearly. She held her composure against that threat despite knowing that every word that would soon come from Dad's mouth would be a lie.

Dad, though, was a different story. He looked like he'd just soiled his shorts and hoped no one could smell the stench. I saw the first bead of sweat appear on his forehead.

Tina had Dad introduce himself, spell his name, and confirm that he was indeed the father of Christina, Daniel, and William Meacham. She then got into her questions.

"Since his auto accident, how many times have you seen your son Billy in the last five weeks?" she asked.

"Every day," Dad said. "Until last week, that is."

"And what occurred last week?"

"My other son Danny told me to leave Billy's place and not come back."

"And why would he tell you that?"

"Objection," Havenhurst said. "The witness can't speak to motive."

"Unless the witness was specifically told the motive," Tina countered.

"Overruled," the judge said.

Confidently, Tina asked Dad the question again. "Why were you told to leave and not come back to see your youngest son?"

"Because I told Danny that I saw Billy blink," Dad said, looking down at his thumbs that I could see he was twiddling.

I turned to Havenhurst, hoping he'd object or something. He patted my arm and whispered, "Let's give them some rope before we string them up by it."

I didn't like that, especially since Dad and Tina were putting lies in my mouth now. But Havenhurst was the lawyer, so I went with it.

"And did you?" Tina asked Dad.

"Did I what?" Dad asked. He seemed like he'd forgotten what they were talking about.

"Did you see your son Billy blink?" Tina asked.

Dad opened his mouth to answer, but no sound came out. He looked at me. I stared back at him through my blackened and bruised eyes. We both knew the truth. He turned to Tina. Her eyes started to bulge, urging him to get on with their scripted lie.

Dad glanced over to the judge. Jacobson gave him a blank look that could have been read as skepticism, boredom, or annoyance.

"What did you say?" Dad asked Tina. His voice had gone weak.

Tina spoke slower as she asked, "Did you see your son Billy blink?"

Dad tilted his head back, staring at the cream-colored ceiling. He took a deep breath and lowered his head. Dad closed his eyes and exhaled all of the air in his lungs before he finally spoke in a voice barely louder than a whisper.

"I wish I had."

23

WHOA! FOR THE FIRST TIME in my life, Dad had done the right thing.

I wasn't sure who was more surprised, Tina or me. Either way, his moment of ethical purity had broken Tina's cool demeanor. She went to her table and frantically searched through her papers before grabbing one.

"I have a sworn affidavit here—"

Dad cut her off. "Baby girl, I don't want to go to jail. As much as I wish I could say he has, Billy hasn't moved once since his accident."

"Objection!" Tina shouted.

"You're objecting to your own witness?" Judge Jacobson asked.

Tina stammered, struggling to find the words. This morning was full of family firsts.

Havenhurst was on his feet, filling the void.

"Your honor, in light of the witness's testimony and what we heard earlier from Dr. Pettis, I'd like to request judgment in favor of the respondent."

"Agreed, counselor," Judge Jacobson said. "I'm

dismissing the petitioner's request. The witness is excused."
She looked down at Tina. "But you, counselor, I'll see you
in chambers immediately."

Havenhurst turned to me and offered his hand. "Told
ya. Bulletproof."

"Yeah, thanks," I said, shaking his hand with not as
much enthusiasm as he had.

Dad came past me as he made his way off the stand. He
wouldn't look at me. Not even to ask what had happened
to my face. He appeared ashamed for what he'd done.

"Dad…" I said, but trailed off as he neared me. I wasn't
sure what else I could or should say.

He looked me in the eye. There was something there I
hadn't seen in him before. Was it guilt? Maybe remorse?

I couldn't tell. Dad didn't have the words for me
either. He nodded to me and continued out of the
courtroom. For some reason, I felt like a total prick right
then and there. Havenhurst was over talking to one of the
ladies who worked for the judge. Judge Jacobson had left
the bench. I guessed she'd gone back to her chambers,
where she would deal with my sister.

Tina stood alone at the table beside mine. She gathered
her things and headed back to face Judge Jacobsen, and
whatever punishment awaited her.

"Tina," I said.

She spun on me like she was ready to slug me with all
of her might. "You know what, Danny? You're the one
who deserves to go to hell."

Clutching her briefcase, Tina headed back to the judge's chambers.

Why had I even tried to bother with her? What did it matter? Did I really think I could win my sister over? I'd done what Billy had wanted. Tina and Dad were against me. Mom wouldn't speak up. At least I had the law on my side.

But if that was the case, why did I feel worse than I had before?

24

"DIDN'T GO SO WELL, HUH?" Veronica asked as I entered from the garage. She'd learned to read my expressions pretty damn well the last month. Either that or my feelings were just plain obvious.

"Oh, it did," I said. "I won."

She looked at me with skepticism. "I wouldn't have guessed it. But maybe it's just the way your face looks right now."

"Yeah, I'm not going to pick up any modeling contracts, am I?"

"And your stripping career is probably sidelined for at least a couple of weeks."

"The good news just doesn't stop. My mom go home?"

"She said she was going home to shower and change, then was going to a meeting, but would be back after."

Was it me, or did it seem like Mom had been going to a lot of meetings lately?

Veronica stepped closer and put her hand on my upper arm. "What's wrong?"

I looked down at Billy then answered, "I don't know. What if Tina's right? What if he only needs another week or so, or even a month?"

"It's always possible," she said. "Is that what you think?"

I thought it over for a while. The answer wasn't coming like before.

"It's so weird," I said. "Why the hell am I having second thoughts about this now?"

"Because you're a normal human being."

"I don't think normal is a word anyone's ever used to describe me."

"Well, you're not some psychotic who wants to go out and kill people to get his jollies."

"I don't even like horror movies."

"See?"

"Do you think I'm doing the right thing?"

"You know I'm not going to answer that."

"Yeah, I know. I was just checking."

"Just because the court says Tina can't interfere with you following his medical directive, it doesn't mean you have to do it now. If ever."

I looked at Billy again. He was the shell of the person he'd been. The machines were giving him life, but the life that had been in him seemed to be all gone.

I shook my head. "If Billy was going to wake up, Mom wouldn't have called me to come home. She knew it then. They all did. None of them wanted to admit it, and they still don't. Which is exactly why he chose me."

I felt calm.

The decision had been made.

The hardest parts were now over.

Or so I thought.

PART IV

Pulling the Plug

1

IT'S EASIER THAN YOU THINK to end someone's life.

If you have the right paperwork, that is.

Which I did.

Billy's trust and medical directive were, in the words of the mighty attorney Martin Havenhurst, bulletproof.

A couple of days after the court hearing, I went back over to Loma Linda Hospital to get things moving. It all sounded weird, but once I'd accepted this was indeed the right thing to do, I was able to put my remaining doubts aside to move forward with granting Billy's wish.

Veronica had suggested I bring up organ donation when I met with Billy's doctor, so I did. It had been a well-meaning suggestion on her part that turned into something much more.

"Normally, I'd be excited about organ donation," Dr. Pettis said while she read Billy's medical file from behind her desk. "Unfortunately, your brother's drug abuse was quite extreme."

"That's a nice way to put it," I said.

She handed Billy's file to me. I leafed through it,

having no idea what I was looking for or at.

Dr. Pettis must've been used to this, as she gave me the plain English synopsis of things. "The damage from the chronic abuse to his organs is extensive. We should be able to use some of his tissue, but not his major organs."

"Can't say I'm all that surprised."

"It really is a shame, though, since your brother is a universal donor."

As I mindlessly flipped through the pages, one piece of paper caught my attention. It was from a fertility clinic. I didn't understand the words on it.

"Excuse me," I said, pulling the page from Billy's file. "What does this word mean?"

I held the report up for Dr. Pettis to read, pointing at the word in question.

She squinted to read it and asked, "Azoospermia?"

"Yeah. What's that mean?"

"It means your brother doesn't have a sperm count."

Say what?

I flipped the page around again to take a closer look at it. *Azoospermia.* No sperm count. It was dated April 3, 2003.

I spoke my next thought without realizing I had.

"This isn't right. Billy has a kid."

Dr. Pettis reached across her desk and took the report from me. She read it over carefully, looked at me, and shook her head.

What the hell is going on? If Billy had no sperm, then how did he get Jessie pregnant? If he didn't, then who in the hell is the Kid's father?

I couldn't breathe. I thought I was going to pass out.

That couldn't be the case.

It couldn't be!

Could it?

2

As a rule I always practiced safe sex.

It was one of the things they really drilled home to you as a teenager in the 90s. You didn't want to catch something you couldn't get rid of. And for me, that included a pregnant girl I hooked up with after a gig. That rule had served me well over the last two decades. It had protected both my sexual health—as Target called it—and what little funds were in my checking account from unwanted child support payments.

I'd only ignored that rule at one time in my life. That was with Jessie.

Now, it hadn't started out that way. She'd started like every other girl I'd had sex with. I met her during a gig, this one at the Brandin' Iron. I'd seen her on the dance floor and she approached me when I went to the bar to get a water from my favorite bartender, Bryon. We chatted a little bit and she asked me to dance. I wasn't the best two-stepper, but I never refused a girl who wanted to dance. It usually meant she wanted more.

It turned out that Jessie knew who I was. She was from

Norco too and had graduated four years behind me. Jessie had seen the first iteration of my band the Regulators back when she was a freshman. She was happy to hear for herself that we'd gotten much better since then.

Jessie come out that night with a guy she was seeing, but he was more interested in playing pool with his buddies than dancing and spending time with her. When he noticed that Jessie was giving me her attention, he and his buddies tried to start some crap with me. Fortunately I was friends with the bouncers who quickly helped Mr. Pool Player and his friends their way out the door.

Since Jessie lived in Norco, I offered her a ride home. We went to Denny's for a post-gig breakfast with the band first. Then I drove her back to Norco, where she lived with her mom. Parked out front of the house was the first time I ever kissed Jessie Patanoe. And man she was quite the kisser. I figured we'd fool around in the car for a bit, but she invited me in. Her mom was open-minded about Jessie having guys over. Her mom said it was safer for Jessie to do that than sneak around. Her only rule was that Jessie needed to keep it down.

Just as we'd had instant chemistry at the bar, Jessie and I had instant chemistry in the bed. There was something that immediately clicked between the two of us in every aspect of our lives. What free time we had, we spent together. When my band played, she was there. When the gig was over, we went back to her mom's house and Jessie's room.

About six months into it, Jessie told me that she was on

birth control and didn't see the point of using condoms. Besides, she said it would feel much better for both of us without them. Being that we'd been together and exclusive for half a year, I said goodbye to the jimmy hats.

Jessie was the only woman I'd ever done that with. I'd never thought that had been a mistake. Until my meeting with Dr. Pettis, that was.

But maybe the report was wrong. Maybe it was mistaken about Billy.

That was something I had to find out.

I drove to Circle K, hoping that Billy's Sometimes-Girl, Kaitlyn was working. I saw the crappy Ford he'd bought her in the parking lot. Going inside, I found her removing overcooked hot dogs from the stainless-steel rolling warmer. I wasn't sure exactly how to say what I'd come to ask, so I stood there. She must've sensed my presence, as after a moment, she turned to face me.

Seeing my black and blue face, Kaitlyn recoiled. "I'm not sure who did that to you, but I'm sure you deserved it for something."

I didn't know how to respond to that, so I let her remark slide. "Look... I need to ask you something," I said, but still didn't know precisely what to ask. "When you and Billy... When you two were intimate... what type of birth control did you use?"

Kaitlyn looked at me with disgust. "What kind of a perv are you?"

"I know it sounds weird... but did you and Billy use

protection?"

"What I do with my body is my business, not yours."

"You're right. But what I need to know is, was he ever concerned about getting you pregnant?"

"Look, you're in charge at Billy's, but I'm in charge here, and I have the right to refuse service to anyone. So I'm going to ask you nicely once to get the hell out of here."

"Okay. I'll leave, but please just answer me this. Did Billy ever say anything to you about not being able to have kids?"

I could tell she was ready to get louder and more insistent about my leaving. That's why I added, "Please. I really need to know."

3

THE LAST TIME I'D BEEN to Jessie's house—technically her mom's house—was the day I found out.

It was a Saturday morning. Sergio, Lonnie, Geoff, and I had returned from our tour in the middle of the night. I got a few hours of sleep at Serg's then went over to surprise Jessie. I'd been miserable on the road without her. The emptiness I felt inside never eased and I knew that I wanted her in my life fully. I had an engagement ring that I'd bought from a pawn shop in Nashville in my pocket.

The surprise she had for me, though, was bigger than the one I had for her. When she opened the door that morning, the shock of seeing me standing there was apparent. But it didn't go away. Her stomach was bigger, but it took a few seconds for me to realize it wasn't because she was fatter. It was because Jessie was pregnant.

My first thought was that she'd somehow gotten pregnant before I left. But why hadn't she gotten a hold of me? I quickly found out when a beat up Honda Civic pulled into the driveway and Billy got out.

"Hey, bro," he said without a trace of any guilt. "I

didn't know you were back."

My eyes burned with tears and rage. I glared at Jessie. Tears were in her eyes too.

"Danny," she said. "I'm sorry."

I turned my back on them and stormed back to my car. My life in Norco ended that day. The next morning, I set off for Nashville on my own.

And now, twelve years later, here I stood in the one place I never thought I'd be again—on Jessie's mom's porch ringing the doorbell.

Jessie opened the door, but the screen door still separated us.

"What do you want?" she asked. She didn't seem angry this time. More like tired.

"To talk," I said.

"It's Mason you should talk to."

I took a deep breath. "It's Mason we need to talk about."

"What's there to talk about?"

I held the fertility report up to the screen door. Jessie leaned forward and tried to read it through the minuscule holes in the mesh. She couldn't and opened the screen door to take the paper from me.

"What is this?" she asked as she read the report.

"Exactly what it says it is."

"What does this mean? Azoo…"

"Azoospermia." I'd gotten good at pronouncing it over the last few hours, then answered the next question I knew she'd ask. "It means Billy's sterile."

As she processed my words, her confusion visibly changed to what might be described as shock, but I detected a touch of fear.

"No, he's not," she said.

"Yeah, he is. His doctor says it's very common for people with a long history of hardcore drug use."

Jessie's eyes never came off the report.

"But Mason was born in 2006..." She couldn't finish the thought.

"I know."

We stood quietly there on her mom's porch, each looking off at something else, neither of us having the courage to face the other.

It was Jessie who ended our momentary silence.

"I guess it finally puts that question to rest."

What? There had been some question in this matter?

I struggled for words. "You mean... you knew I might be the... I mean his..."

That was all I could manage to get out. I couldn't say the word. I thought the weight of this had hit me sitting with Dr. Pettis. No. It happened here on the front porch.

Jessie finally made eye contact with me. A tear fell from her left eye, and she nodded, before casting her eyes to the ground as more tears came.

"I'd already missed my period before Billy and I got together."

That information sat between us. It appeared that last

time with me, the night of our fight, the night before I left on tour, had been the moment.

Jessie wiped the tears from her eyes. "I always wondered why he didn't have any kids with any of the other girls he was with, because he wasn't as careful about it. I guess he knew he didn't need to be."

"Yeah."

She raised the one-page report and studied its information again. "Why'd he even get tested for this?" she asked.

"It was long before he hit the Lotto. I remember he got his first DUI on New Year's of '03. He said he was going to hire a lawyer and fight it. I told him he'd need money for that. Guess he was trying to get the money when he found out, 'cause he wound up with a public defender."

Jessie sat down on the steps. She spoke, but her words didn't seem directed at me.

"But it makes no sense. The way he loves Mason... the way he wanted me back... how bad he wanted the three of us to be a family..." She raised her head and asked, "Why would he do any of that if Mason wasn't his son?"

I shrugged. "Maybe he didn't believe the results. Maybe he didn't want to." I looked down at her. "It's not like he had any reason to believe otherwise."

"There was always a chance Mason was his."

"But if you'd even suspected that he was mine..."

"I was twenty-two. I was pregnant and scared. And

you weren't here."

"I would've been if you told me."

"And do you think that would have really changed anything?"

"What do you mean? It would've changed everything."

"How exactly would that conversation have gone? 'Danny, I'm pregnant, and there's a decent chance you're the father... but still, you should also know I had sex with Billy after Tina's graduation party, so there's a chance it's him.'"

She was right. I would still have hated them both. But...

"If I'd known I was the responsible one—"

"Listen to yourself. You can't bring yourself now to say the word *father*. And even if nothing had happened between me and Billy, you wouldn't have wanted me to keep Mason."

"That's not true. There's no way you could know that."

"Danny, I know you. You would've seen him as an obstacle to your career."

She was right. I looked down at the steps and mindlessly kicked at the chipped edge of the top one. I could hear her sobbing behind me. I turned back to her. Tears covered Jessie's cheeks.

"God, what am I supposed to tell Mason?" she said.

"Why would you tell him anything?" I said. She

looked up at me again, searching for more, and I provided it. "Billy's always been his dad. There's no reason to change that now."

"Thank you," Jessie said. "Mason loves Billy more than you can imagine."

I didn't have to imagine. I'd seen that love in the Kid's eyes at Circle K a couple of days ago. And felt it in his solid uppercut to my crotch as well.

Jessie smiled through her tears. I slowly moved over and sat down on the step beside her. She continued to cry, and I did something I hadn't done in forever and never thought I'd do again. I put my arm around Jessie's shoulder. She leaned into me, letting the tears fall harder.

"Danny, I'm so sorry. About everything."

I didn't bristle at the sound of those words I so hated. For some bizarre reason, it felt to me that she sincerely meant them.

My phone rang at that moment. I pulled it out to silence it but saw the caller was Veronica. The entire time she'd been Billy's nurse, she'd only texted me. She'd never called.

"It's Billy's nurse. I gotta answer this."

I picked up and didn't even say hello.

"Hey. Everything all right?"

"Not exactly," Veronica said.

"'Kay. What is it?"

"First of all, it's not Billy. It's your mom."

4

THE GOOD NEWS WAS MOM didn't have a major heart attack or stroke or anything like that.

The bad news was she had come back to Billy's with a Texas-sized bottle of Jack Daniels.

While this wasn't officially any of Veronica's business, she did me a solid by calling. I left Jessie and rushed back to Billy's. Jess had enough to think over and didn't need me hanging around anymore. I was sure we'd be talking about this recent paternal discovery again before too long.

Veronica came into the garage as I got out of the Supra. "She's in watching TV," she told me.

"Is she drunk?"

"I don't think so. I can't tell how much she's had."

We went inside. Veronica headed back over to Billy and I went into the family room. I found Mom sitting on the sofa. The TV was on without any sound. Sitting on the coffee table in front of her was the bottle of Jack Daniel's.

A glass with melting ice in it sat beside the bottle. There didn't seem to be any residue of the whiskey in the glass. Looking closer, I could see the cap of the JD was still sealed.

"What you watching?" I asked Mom.

I didn't startle her, so she'd obviously noticed me come inside. "Nothing. I've just been thinking."

"About drinking?" I asked, moving over to the sofa.

"I was on my way to a meeting and I wanted one damn cigarette. I went into the liquor store to get a pack, but I wondered what the man working there would think of me, and I didn't want to be like that lady with the hole in her throat in those commercials, so I bought this instead."

"Can't say that either is much of a good idea."

"How come I could stop and Billy couldn't?" she asked. There weren't any tears in her eyes, but the pain she felt was deep and real. "He had far bigger scares than I did. I only had the heart attack. How come that was enough to make me stop and he couldn't stay sober?"

"I don't know. Everyone's different."

"But if I'd been sober... maybe he never would've started."

"Now that's Dad talking."

"It doesn't mean he's wrong."

That was easily the nicest thing she'd said about Dad since... well, since long before I could remember. I considered making a joke of it, but Mom would probably take it wrong at that point. I went with the truth.

"I don't recall you forcing liquor or pills or anything else down his throat."

"He still learned it all from watching me."

"Did he? I saw the same things he did, and I don't touch any of it."

"Like I told you, you've always been the strong one."

"That had nothing to do with it. I stayed sober because I hated Billy. I didn't want to be anything like him. So I promised myself I wouldn't drink, smoke weed, or take anything else."

It was the truth. I'd never admitted it to anyone, but that was why. And what did any of it really matter, given what I'd learned that day?

"The irony is," I said, "while I was focused on making sure I didn't become anything that resembled him... when I wasn't looking, I turned out being just like Dad."

"You are nothing like your father," Mom said sternly.

"No. I'm exactly like him."

"Oh, you think so?"

"Without getting into detail, yeah, I know so."

A crazy part of me wanted to blurt out those details, but fortunately, Mom spoke before I could.

"Let me tell you a little story," she said. "When I gave birth to Billy, he was several weeks early. It was scarier than hell. We didn't know if he was going to make it."

"I don't remember that."

"Of course you don't. You were barely two years old. Aunt Geena came and took care of you and Tina while I was in the hospital with Billy. And do you know where your father was most of that time?"

"In the waiting room watching the Angels?"

"I wish. At least he'd have been at the hospital." She looked me dead in the eye. "He was out playing gigs with his band all night and sleeping most of the day."

That sounded way too familiar.

"I know you didn't mean to, but you pretty much just proved my point," I said.

"No. When I called you about Billy's accident, you came home."

"I can't say it was because I wanted to."

"But you still did. And you've been by your brother's side, taking care of him every day since."

"Only because Tina guilted me into it."

"I don't buy it."

"Well, it's the truth."

"If it is, then why didn't you let Tina have her way? Why didn't you make her Billy's agent? Why did you fight her in court to make sure Billy's wishes were followed?"

"You really want to know why? Because after everything Billy did to me, after every way he ruined my life, I really wanted him to wake up from this."

"You see? You do care for your brother."

"That's not why. I wanted Billy to wake up and see me here and know that I really am better than him. And maybe, for the first time in his miserable life, he'd appreciate me."

Wow.

I didn't know where that came from, but again my

words were the truth.

"If you didn't care for him, Danny, that wouldn't matter to you."

I was quiet. What Mom said made sense, but how could it be possible that, after all those years of hatred toward him, that I could possibly love the Prick?

Mom continued, "And whether you know it or not, Danny, you are a very good man."

I couldn't say it, but no, I wasn't. I'd driven Jessie from me with my self-centered attitude. I'd never known my own son. And I'd disowned my brother, who had taken care of my kid for years and never said a word about it. I'd blown up my band. I'd skipped my best friend's wedding. I'd avoided my family. I'd wrecked every important relationship in my life.

"No, Mom," I said. "I'm actually a pretty big asshole."

"Then you are clearly part of the right family."

Her comment gave me a much-needed chuckle.

Mom smiled. "Why don't you grab a glass, and you and I can be drunk assholes together?"

"Mom… I don't drink."

"That's right. And neither do I."

Mom lifted herself from the sofa, grabbed the bottle of JD, and went into the kitchen. I watched as she broke the seal then poured the liquor down the drain.

5

Is there a heaven?

Is there a hell?

John Lennon sang that you can imagine there isn't either, but it's not that simple, even if you can. Especially if you're the person put in charge of ending someone's life. It gets even more complicated when the person in question is a royal screw-up, like Billy. Sergio had assured me that Billy was *saved*, but was that really enough? I wasn't even exactly sure what that meant.

"Hey," I said, lightly tapping a knuckle on Sergio's office door. The church had been open but was empty inside, so I'd found my way to the back office.

"Come on in," he said, turning away from his computer.

I did but didn't sit in one of the chairs. I didn't know how long I'd be there.

"Your face hurt?" he asked.

"Yeah, but I think it looks worse than it actually feels."

"I guess that's good."

"Yeah. Anyway, things went my way in court," I said.

"I heard."

"Tina tell you?"

"Your mom. She asked if I'd do the service."

"He's not even dead yet. Not officially."

"You thinking about waiting a little longer?"

I shook my head. "His doctor's coming over to remove the feeding tube and the ventilator this afternoon."

"But you're not sure whether that's the right thing to do."

"No… it's just… I feel bad. And scared."

"If you didn't, I'd be worried about you."

Sergio meant well, but it made me feel even more anxious.

"Yeah… well… I should probably get back, but if you're not busy, maybe you could come by and say a prayer or something."

"What time?"

"Two."

"I'll be there."

"Thanks. I'm sure my mom will appreciate that."

I turned for the door and stopped when he said, "Danny." I looked back at my friend as he stood. "Would you like me to pray with you?"

The words that came out of my mouth surprised me.

"Would you?"

6

WHEN I STOPPED BY CHARLIE Purkiss's house, Dad didn't hide from me. He let me in.

It was a nice house. You could tell at one point it had been decorated with a woman's touch, but slowly the place was being changed due to the male dominance over the years. Dad took me back to his room, which was little more than a bedroom with housing his guitars, much like mine.

There was another Fender Stratocastor, a red one, alongside a Telecaster. Next to them sat a Martin acoustic guitar I knew Dad loved, the Univox he'd allowed me to learn on as a kid, and his one Gibson, a classic Les Paul.

I turned my attention from the guitars to Dad. "Thanks for telling the truth in court the other day."

"I didn't want to lie… It's just…"

"I know. Tina can be a little overbearing."

Dad looked at me as if I didn't understand what he couldn't say.

I amended my statement. "Right. She can be *a lot* overbearing."

He started to say something, stopped, then said, "Is that what you came by to say?"

"That and uh... they're going to come over and turn the machines off this afternoon."

"So you're going to go through with it after all?"

"It's what Billy wants."

He looked away from me. "I know. I know."

"Anyway, if you want to come over, you can."

"Thanks, but... I don't want to watch that happen."

"I understand."

"You were right the other day. Billy's already gone. And I've made my peace with that."

"Okay. If you change your mind, let me know."

I didn't know what to do. If he were Mom, I'd hug him. But Dad and I didn't hug. Should I shake his hand? That was our normal hello and goodbye ritual but seemed too impersonal now. Seeing him vulnerable like this made me want to dig something deeper out of him if I could. So I did.

"Dad, can I ask you something totally out of left field?"

"Shoot."

"When you found out Mom was pregnant with Tina, how did you feel?"

"Honestly?"

"Please."

"It scared the hell out of me. I'm pretty sure she felt that same way."

"And was Mom being pregnant the only reason you

married her?"

"Of course not. I loved her."

"You did?"

"You may find this impossible to believe, Danny Boy, but your mother is the only woman I ever truly loved."

I really couldn't believe my ears. "Then how did you fall out of love with her?"

"I haven't." The look on my face must have told Dad I needed more of an answer than that, and he continued, "Just because I can't love her the way she wants to be loved doesn't mean that I don't."

"The way you two fought—hell, the way you two still do—I figured you never wanted to be married or have a family."

"I wouldn't say that. Some men just aren't cut out to be husbands... or, as you've pointed out, fathers."

Ouch.

That was now a point that I didn't like hearing said back to me.

"I was mad when I said that," I told him.

"You were still right."

We stood silently in his room, surrounded by his guitars.

"Danny Boy, if I could go back and do it different, I probably would. But too much time has passed. That ship has long since sunk."

7

WAITING FOR THE DOORBELL TO ring so you can let the doctor in who's going to pull the plug on your brother seemed like waiting for the Grim Reaper to come and, well, I guess, reap.

Mom had called and texted Tina. She didn't respond. Mom suggested I do the same, but that would be meaningless. If Tina wasn't answering Mom, she sure as hell wouldn't answer me. I did, however, reach out to Jessie and let her know that she and Mason were welcome to come by.

And when the doorbell did ring, it turned out to be Jessie standing there, not Dr. Pettis. But she was alone.

"You didn't bring Mason?" I asked.

"He's in the car. He doesn't want to come in if you're here."

Over Jessie's shoulder, I could see Mason sitting in the passenger seat of a Subaru parked on the street right in front of the house. Mason gave, or pretended to give, all of his attention to whatever electronic device he held in his hands.

"Can't say I blame him," I said. "You know, I can take off for a while—"

Jessie put her hand on my arm, stopping me from saying more. "Why don't you go and talk to him?"

What would he want to say to me? Or what could I say to him?

"Hi, I was right, I'm not your uncle, I'm really your dad, but I'm also a total douchebag, so I never knew it, and I've spent my life resenting you, but maybe we can play catch sometime?"

"That's probably not a good idea," I said.

"I think it is. For both of you." She looked me in the eyes. It was like the first night I was with her. Something told me she was right. I nodded and let her into the house as I stepped out.

I went out to Jessie's Subaru. The window was rolled down. Mason acted as if he didn't notice me. He didn't have any earbuds in, so he must've heard the crunch of the dirt and rocks under my feet as I approached. I stood before his door and watched him for a while. He still ignored me.

"Hey there," I finally said.

Without looking up from his game, Mason reached a hand over to the door, and the car door's window mechanically slid up. This was useless. I'd go for a walk. Jessie could get the Kid in to see Billy.

No. Not the Kid.

My kid.

My son.

I took a chance and pulled the handle for the back door. The door opened. I slid in behind Mason, occupying the spot between the two rear seats so I could see him in the space between the two front ones.

"Should've locked the doors too," I said, trying to make light of the moment. Mason didn't laugh or acknowledge me, but his back visibly stiffened, and his concentration on the game seemed to intensify.

"I can't say I blame you for now wanting to be around me," I said. I wasn't sure where to go from there. Mason didn't give me any cues. He definitely remained pissed at me for what had happened at Circle K.

"I was under a lot of pressure," I said. "I was mad. You ran into me at exactly the wrong moment, and I unloaded on you. Not because you deserved it. Just because you were there."

Mason kept playing his game. I had no clue if I was getting through to him or not. Probably not. Stubbornness must truly be a Meacham genetic trait. What else could I say? I reached for the door handle to exit. That's when he spoke.

"You're right, though. My dad's a pretty big fuck-up."

Yeah, I really am. More than you know.

But he wasn't referring to me. He was referring to Billy. I had to respond. Mason had opened the door a crack, albeit a small one. I had to see if I could get it opened up a bit further or he might slam it shut on me forever.

"My brother made a lot of bad choices in his life," I said. "But guess what? So have I."

I leaned forward, hoping to get Mason to face me. He didn't, but I kept going.

"The truth is, we all make mistakes. Some big. Some small. But I'm starting to think it's what we learn from them that actually matters."

Still not looking at me, Mason said, "If my dad had learned from any of his, maybe he wouldn't be like he is now."

He couldn't have had a clue about what he was saying, yet he was spot-on about me. As Sergio had been. For twelve years I'd been running from the pain of my past, hoping it would go away and I'd never get hurt again. I had two options. Keep running or stand still and face it.

Screw it.

I was tired of running.

"Your dad…" I said, and paused. My instinct to climb out of the car and run down the road kicked in.

No.

Not this time.

"Your dad might've been a bit slow to figure things out. But trust me when I tell you that he knows how badly he screwed things up. And if there was any way he could make them right, I know he absolutely would."

Mason finally broke off from his game. His eyes went to the rearview mirror and he looked back to me. I could see he was hurt in the reflection. For very similar but different reasons, he was feeling exactly the same thing I was. I held his stare and continued.

"Mason... I know I'll never be able to replace my brother in your life. But I would like a chance to at least be your uncle... if I can. And if you're good with that, I promise I'll never talk to you like the way I did again."

We stared at each other in the mirror for a long time. Mason then turned around to face me. I leaned forward, wondering what he would say. He stuck out his right hand, clenching his fist while extending his pinky finger.

"Swear?" he asked.

"Yeah. But you've got to promise me you'll never sock me in the family jewels again."

Mason smiled. "Deal."

I reached out my hand, wrapped his pinky in mine, and we shook on it. I closed my eyes, hoping not to cry as I held my son's hand for the first time in my life.

8

TWENTY MINUTES LATER, I STOOD next to Mom, holding her aging hand with Sergio on her other side. Jessie and Mason were on the other side of Serg. We all watched in silence as Dr. Pettis and Veronica turned off the machines and detached the tubes connected to them from Billy's body.

A weird silence hung over the room. The low hum of the machines that had been whirling nonstop since Billy's return now fell quiet. We all held our breath, too, which I was sure contributed to the awkwardness.

"So, what happens now?" I asked.

"It all depends," Dr. Pettis said. "Some pass in a couple of days. Others remain for a couple weeks."

"In other words, we'll just have to wait and see."

"Yes."

"Well, that's pretty much been the standard operating procedure since I got here."

Mom squeezed my hand, backed away, and sat down in the comfy chair.

Mason and Jessie cried and clutched each other tightly.

She decided they'd seen enough. I walked them to the door, but there was nothing to say. Their tears said it all.

Dr. Pettis left too and told me how I could get hold of her anytime.

It was just me, Mom, Sergio, and Veronica left there with Billy. Sergio knelt down by the comfy chair and talked quietly to Mom. I went over to Veronica.

"I can stay for a while if you want," Veronica said.

"No, it's all right. I think your work here is done. But thank you for... well, for everything."

Veronica gave me a big, unexpected hug. I held to her tight and she felt great against me. But it wasn't sexual. It was person to person. A genuine human connection between me and a woman. I'd forgotten how good it felt. Guess I'd needed that more than I'd let myself believe.

9

UNLIKE ME, BILLY NEVER CARED about other people or their opinions. He always did things his own way. Even in his unconscious state, without anything artificially keeping him alive, his rebellious spirit wouldn't allow him to pass quickly. I found it strangely emboldening. I'd always run from things. Billy, on the other hand, right or wrong—most often wrong—always stood his ground and fought. Even now.

Mom and I only left his side to use the bathroom and to grab something to eat or drink. Neither of us showered or went to bed. We wanted to be there with him.

After two days of that, I was beat. And Mom was in far worse shape.

"You need to get some sleep," I told her.

"So do you."

That was true, but not as much as she did. "I'm good for a few more hours," I said. "Why don't you crash out in Mason's room?"

"You'll wake me if..."

"Yeah."

Mom got up, kissed Billy on the cheek, and went into Mason's room.

After she closed the door, I moved my chair closer to Billy's bed.

He could be gone at any moment. If ever there was a time for me to say something to my brother, this was it. Yet the words would not come. Other than telling Billy what to go do with or to himself, I still had no idea what to say to him.

Thanks for taking care of my son?

That seemed like an appropriate thing to say, but I didn't think I'd ever thanked Billy for anything. At least not non-sarcastically.

Why didn't you tell anyone?

That was the question I'd carry with me for the rest of my life. I guessed Jessie would too.

Did you really love her after all? Was that why you got with her?

I never would've imagined asking such questions or even entertaining those thoughts before. Still, Jessie believed Billy had loved her and questioned that I had.

Did I ever really love Jessie?

Of course I did!

Jessie couldn't have hurt me like she did if I hadn't loved her. She simply didn't know it.

Maybe, just like Dad, I couldn't love Jessie the way she wanted to be loved.

But Billy could?

It made no sense at all.

A knock at the door rescued me from those thoughts. No one was expected. At this late hour, it had to be one of Billy's stoner friends. I wasn't sure I'd let them in. I had no interest in dealing with Eric Parker or Bald Tommy. However, if Kaitlyn was with them, maybe I would let them in. I at least owed her that.

But when I opened the front door it wasn't any of them. Instead, I found Tina standing there.

"Hey, little brother," she said meekly.

"Hey," I said, not moving to let her in. She had to have an agenda for being here. Tina always had an agenda.

"I kinda lost it lately, didn't I?"

That was an understatement. "Yeah, you went pretty Richter."

"Can I come in?"

I took a chance, stepped back and let her inside. She went straight to Billy's bed. The tears came immediately as she looked down upon his dying body. I took up a position opposite her on the other side of the bed.

She looked at me and said, "I'm not mad at you for following Billy's wishes. It's just... I didn't... I just don't want him to die."

"I know," I said. "Neither do I."

10

T<small>INA AND</small> I <small>SAT TOGETHER</small> with Billy into the early morning hours as dawn neared. She did her best to lighten things up by telling funny stories about Billy from when we were growing up. Her stories, oddly enough, depressed me.

"You know what sucks?" I said. "You want to know what bothers me the most? I don't have stories like you do about him."

"I'm sure you do."

"Nope. I can remember every shitty thing he ever did to me, but I don't have one single good memory of anything."

"There has to be something."

"I've tried coming up with one the last few days, and I can't."

Tina thought for a bit then said, "What about the night we TPed the Galiffas'?"

"We did?" I knew the Galiffas but had no clue what she was talking about. They lived a block over from us on Hillside. As kids, we'd sometimes go over during the summer to swim in their doughboy pool.

"Yeah," Tina's said. "I'd just gotten my license, and Billy wanted to go TPing, but I was afraid we'd get caught—"

"And I suggested the Galiffas' house…" The memory slowly crept up out of the basement corner in my mind.

"Because even if they caught us…"

"… Mrs. Galiffa would never call the cops," we said at the same time.

"I totally forgot about that." I started laughing as the images of that teenage misadventure screened in the theater of my mind. Tina had driven us up to Ranchland and bought an eight-pack of toilet paper, then we headed over to the Galiffas'. It was late, or probably early in the morning, and the family would be asleep. We'd also picked their house because they had plenty of trees and bushes. We were doing a great job of decorating their front yard in white biodegradable streamers when things turned to shit.

Literally for Billy.

"You know, I saw him fall in," I said.

"You did? I only heard the splash."

"He was walking backward unspooling a roll from between his fingers, and just like that, he disappeared. I didn't know what happened to him. Then the stench hit me."

"Oh my God, it was horrible," Tina said. "Who has an open septic tank in their front yard?"

"The Galiffas, obviously."

"Billy was so mad."

"Yeah, but he kept his mouth shut the whole time."

"Probably safer that way."

"If I'd fallen in, I would've been screaming."

"Not Billy."

"He had to throw his clothes away in the neighbor's trash can because you wouldn't let him in the car."

"Uck!" Tina said, her face scrunched up as she relived that revolting moment. "He was covered in sewage!"

"I remember. But do you remember we had to go back the next day because he'd left his wallet in his pants?"

"That's right! And their neighbor came out wanting to know why Billy was digging through his trash."

"Billy thought that guy was going to shoot him!"

"Right! But Billy found his wallet and we got out there."

"Oh, and his wallet stunk too."

"It smelled like the septic tank."

I laughed. "I remember calling him Shit Boy for weeks."

We shared a hard laugh at our younger brother's misfortune. It was a good laugh. I couldn't recall honestly laughing like that since I'd retuned home. We were laughing so hard that neither of us noticed Billy's breathing had stopped.

I picked up on it first. Something didn't sound right. No, that wasn't it. Something didn't *feel* right. I stood and looked down into the bed. Billy's chest no longer moved up and down.

Tina got up, reached out, and grabbed my hand. I put my free hand down and stretched my index finger out under Billy's nose to see if there was even a trace of air coming out of him.

There wasn't.

I touched Billy's neck, looking for a pulse.

There wasn't one.

I turned to Tina and shook my head. She leaned down and sweetly kissed Billy's forehead as her tears started.

"Goodbye, baby brother," she said. "I love you."

I looked away from my sister the second I felt the warm tears on my cheeks, and I wept for the loss of my younger brother Billy.

11

WHILE I'D NEVER BEEN DRUNK, stoned, high, or intoxicated in any manner, the next few days were probably the closest comparable experience I could have. I recollect small bits and pieces of everything that happened, but not completely. The images were blurry and the sounds garbled.

I was sitting in the big, comfy chair in Billy's living room when my clarity returned. The room looked completely different before. The past four weeks, it had literally been Billy's hospital room. Not anymore.

The hospital bed and the machines had been removed. I had yet to move the regular furniture back to their proper places. The room had a big, empty spot where the bed had been; impressions from its wheels and those of the life support machines had sunk into the carpet. That more or less described how I felt. Empty, with deep imprints into me that may or may not go away.

"Can I get your sig on these?" Veronica asked, pulling me out of my thoughts. She'd come by to supervise the removal of the bed and equipment two days after Billy passed. The funeral home had come for his body the same morning he died.

I took the clipboard and pen she offered. I wrote my signature on all the indicated places without reading any of them. What would the point be in reading them anyway?

Veronica took the clipboard and pen back from me, then said, "Well, that's it for me. You feel like grabbing a bite?"

"Nah. I'm all right," I said.

"Okay, but for the record, I just asked you out, and you turned me down."

"Wow. I guess I'm slipping."

"So it would appear."

A week ago, I would have been all over getting a bite with Veronica. Then all over her. But I had completely missed the opening she'd finally provided.

"I've got a lot on my mind," I said, and it was true.

"Apparently."

"My mom wants me to speak at the funeral tomorrow. I have no idea what I'm going to say."

"I'm sure you'll come up with something."

"Saying nice things about Billy isn't something I've had much practice at."

"Let the words come out naturally and you'll be fine."

"The last time I tried that, it didn't go so well."

"You'll be fine."

"I hope so. I also hope I can get a rain check on that offer to get a bite."

"We'll see."

"We'll see?"

"Yeah. We'll see."

Veronica left, and I returned to the chair. I'd succeeded at taking down her resistance, and now her rule didn't even apply, but I'd missed my opening. But that wasn't what troubled me.

What was I going to say tomorrow?

What could I say?

I really had nothing.

At that moment, Dad's black Stratocaster caught my eye. Everything that had been brought into the house following Billy's arrival had left, except that guitar. It still sat in its holder next to the little amp.

I grabbed my phone and sent a text to Dad.

Hey Dad. Was that a Martin I saw in your room the other day?

A minute later, his reply came back.

Of course! Best acoustic guitar ever made!

For once there was a solid opinion my father and I shared.

I texted him back.

Any chance I can borrow it?

12

RIVERVIEW COMMUNITY CHURCH WAS PRETTY full that Thursday. Only the last few rows were empty. More people than I expected or could've imagined came out to say their goodbyes to Billy. The front of the sanctuary was filled with flowers and two photo collages of Billy's life that Mom, Tina, and Jessie had spent hours putting together.

I sat beside Mom; Tina sat on her other side. Next to Tina was Mason, then Jessie. Her daughter wasn't with her. Jessie had left her with her mom. Dad sat to the right of me. Aunt Geena and Uncle Jim had come back from Phoenix. They sat behind us, along with cousins I hadn't seen for years.

Various people from growing up, half of whom had gained weight, lost hair, or simply stopped caring about their appearance after graduation, were present. They included Brett Henniker, Kaitlyn—who'd dressed up for the service and looked very attractive—and a few other faces I recognized even if I didn't know their names. Omar was there too. I thought I saw him recording the funeral service with his phone.

Cir-Ass Varg-Ass is in the house.

A dozen or so stoners attended en masse with Eric Parker and Bald Tommy. Somewhere a local dispensary or two probably sat closed in honor of the passing of my brother. Mom had asked Eric to speak as Billy's best friend. I'd been against it, but didn't voice my objections. Even if I bombed there was no way he could upstage me.

Eric told a story about he and Billy and some friends going to see a concert at Universal Amphitheater and what happened after.

"...and Billy said whoever would dive into the water with him, he'd buy their booze for the rest of the weekend, so how could I pass that up? I dived right in behind him. How the hell were we to know the stream was only six inches deep? I was lucky. I belly-flopped, but Billy's teeth went through his lip, and he dislocated his shoulder and messed up his knee real bad. The ambulance took him to the hospital, and when they finally let us back to see him, what's he say to me? 'Guess I'm buying your booze all weekend, you prick.'"

Eric must've noticed the looks on all of our faces, as he quickly apologized for his language.

"Oh, I'm not supposed to say that in church, am I?" He looked to Sergio, sitting nearby. Sergio gave a small shake of his head, but I could also see he was suppressing a smile.

"Sorry," Eric told the mourners. "But you know Billy. He was always up for a good time. And I'm sure up in heaven he's the dude everyone wants to hang with."

Eric paused and looked up at the ceiling. "I look forward to seeing you again, bro. Just not too soon. Peace out."

Eric stepped down from the platform and went back to his seat behind ours. I turned to see Bald Tommy high-five him for his performance.

Sergio returned to the podium and said, "We can all say that, without a doubt, Billy Meacham lived a fun-filled and colorful life. I'd now like to ask Billy's brother Danny to come up and share with us."

Mom squeezed my hand. I stood and walked up on the platform. Looking out, I could see everyone in the pews was tense or concerned about what I might say. I couldn't blame them. Given the history with Billy they all knew I had, I'd be the last person you'd expect to speak at his funeral, much less attend it. Maybe that's why so many people were here, to see if I'd lose it on my younger brother one last time.

I looked at Jessie. She seemed as nervous as anyone. Tina and Mom held hands and their breath. Mason gave me a curious look. In the back, I saw Veronica staring right at me. I hadn't realized she'd come. She was wearing a black dress with a neckline a bit lower than should be worn to a funeral.

How could I be so dense as to miss her invitation to grab a bite yesterday?

Veronica caught me staring at her and gave me a wink. That was all the encouragement I needed to do what I planned on doing.

"Hi," I said into the mic. "I've got a lot of memories of my brother. But as most of you probably know, I can't say it would be a good idea to share many of them in church."

I thought that would get me a laugh and people would relax a little. It didn't and they didn't.

"And you know, I'm not all that good at talking like this, so I'm gonna stick to what I am good at."

I picked up Dad's Martin. I'd miced up the strings and placed it on the stage before the service had begun. The night before, I'd written a song on this guitar. The first song I'd written since throwing in the towel in Nashville. A song I'd written for Billy.

"We were born brothers, but we never became friends
We fought, we screamed, we punched, but never made amends
Over the years the wounds went deep and the pain didn't stop
I wish I'd understood those demons you always fought
I only looked at you through the things you did to me
I didn't understand how hard you were fighting to be free
You were a son, a father, and to so many a friend
I wish we'd talked before you reached your untimely end
As we gather now, forcing smiles through our frowns
There's only one thing I can say, so I hope you're looking
    down
You don't have to say you're sorry
You don't have to say you're sorry
You don't have to say you're sorry anymore."

13

After the funeral, Tina and Sergio's wife Sonia handed out flyers with directions to Billy's house. There would be food and drinks and all the stuff you have at things like that. I wasn't big on the idea of having people over. I was wiped out from that song.

Brett Henniker shook my hand as he exited the church. He'd provided all of the food that would soon be served at no cost to us. He really was a good dude.

"Danny," Brett said. "I'm sorry about your loss."

"Thank you," I told him. "And thanks for putting everything together at the house for us."

"Least I could do, especially for one of April's Fools."

"Well, I appreciate it."

"Did you see Corey Foster's gonna run for Congress?" he asked.

"I always figured he would."

"Too bad he's a Democrat."

"They're not all bad, are they?"

Brett looked at me with suspicion, then said, "No, but since Trump got elected, they've all gone crazy."

"The whole country's gone crazy since the election."

And it had, but I didn't care to talk about politics, especially that day.

Brett went on his way, and many more people stopped by to share their condolences. Omar forced me into taking a selfie with him. He definitely had earned his nickname Circ-Ass Varg-Ass.

Sergio and I were the last people to leave the church.

"Everything was real nice," I told him. "Thanks for putting it together."

"You're welcome," Sergio said as he locked the doors to his church. "That was a heck of a song. I knew you still had it."

"Thanks."

"You better keep writing."

"I think I might."

Sergio pointed a finger in my face. "I didn't say think about it. I said you better keep writing."

"Or what? Will I have to worry about a lightning bolt striking me?"

He shook his head. "That's a bit Old Testament. I'll just figure a way to lock you and Lonnie in a room together and let him take his aggression out on you."

I laughed. "Okay. Okay. You coming over to the house?

"Of course."

14

WHEN I GOT TO BILLY'S, Dad was standing out front talking to Eric Parker, Bald Tommy, and the cadre of stoners. Dad held all of their limited attention as he explained what he considered to be the downfall of rock music.

"I swear to you, the end of rock and roll began the day the Bee Gees hit the charts and culminated on the day that John Bonham died. Without Led Zeppelin, rock and roll was doomed. Absolutely doomed."

My nostrils picked up the distinct odor of what guys Dad's age once called *reefer* as I passed them. At least they weren't smoking in the house. I went through the front door and saw Omar talking excitedly to Tina about something.

Now those two would make an interesting combo.

At least for my entertainment value. Besides, Lard-Ass Circ-Ass Varg-Ass would be better off replacing his Quarter Pounders with some veggie burgers.

I made my way through the house and wound up at the sliding glass door. Outside I found Jessie sitting in a deck chair with sunglasses on, looking out to the pool where Mason swam and played with some other kids.

I went out and sat in the chair next to her.

"Mason doing all right?" I asked.

"He's sad. But he's supposed to be."

"Yeah."

We watched him for a long while, then I said what I had been meaning to all day but couldn't find the right time for it.

"I was thinking about it... and why don't you move in here?"

"Are you being serious or just thinking about loud?"

"Both, I guess. I mean, this place is Mason's when he turns twenty-one anyway, so why don't you two live here?"

"You do know I have a daughter too?"

"Yeah. I meant you three."

"That's sweet, but it's not necessary."

"It's better than leaving it empty or renting it to strangers for the next ten years."

"Tina said you were moving back. Why don't you live here?"

"I'm going to stay with my mom for a while. I don't think it's a good idea that she's alone right now. Besides, there's a lot of tough memories for me here. Maybe you and your kids could start making some good ones."

"How about if I talk to Mason about and get back with you?"

"Works for me."

Jessie leaned over and kissed me on the cheek. It had been forever since her lips touched any part of my body. It was sweet and kind, and I appreciated it.

15

I WENT INSIDE TO GRAB a Diet Dr. Pepper and found that Mom had Veronica cornered in the kitchen. Veronica hadn't seen me enter, so I allowed myself to take a very long look at her.

Wow. That black dress Veronica wore was something else. It easily would've made weaker men openly drool. My imagination had underestimated how striking her curves were under those scrubs.

"Mom," I said as I went to the fridge and got a soda. "You've got a house full of relatives you never see that you could be talking to, but instead, you wind up here with Veronica, who you've seen every day for nearly a month."

"Danny, if any of them were worth talking to, I'd make a point to see them more often than I do."

"Gotta love that brutal honesty," I said.

"I find it refreshing," Veronica said.

"Thank you," Mom said. "And speaking of honesty, Danny, I can't tell you enough how beautiful your song was. Wasn't that song beautiful?" she asked Veronica.

"For an exotic dancer, he's quite the musician."

"What?" Mom asked.

"TMI on her part, Mom," I said.

Mom brought her attention back to me. "You should play the song again."

"Nah. I'm all played out today."

"Just one more time," Mom said.

"That song took a lot out of me."

"Okay, later, then. I'm going to check on Tina."

"Hey," I said, "that guy she's talking to—he's single and available, from what I hear."

"Really?"

I couldn't resist. While Tina had come around since the court hearing, she totally had this coming.

"Oh yeah," I said. "I knew him from high school. They'd probably make an interesting couple."

Mom had a mischievous smile as she walked off, hopefully to play uninvited matchmaker for my sister.

"Your mom's right," Veronica said. "That was quite the song."

"I'm glad you liked it."

"Singer, songwriter, and exotic dancer. You're quite the triple threat."

"You haven't seen half of my talents yet."

"You mean there's more?

"Absolutely."

"Do tell."

"I would, but I have this rule that I never discuss such things with someone who used to work for me until after the first date."

"That's understandable. A person has to have rules."

"They help keep you out of trouble."

"Yes, they do."

I paused briefly then made my move. "Word on the street is that Italian is your favorite type of food."

"Your info is good. You have something in mind?"

"I was thinking that me plus you equals dinner on Saturday night."

"I think that might add up."

"Good 'cause I hear there's this little hole-in-the-wall place in Corona that's fantastic."

Veronica smiled. "I think I've heard the same thing somewhere."

"Then I guess it's a date."

"Yeah. It's a date, Danny Boy."

Mason's Dads

A Prequel Story to Last Wishes

You've heard Danny's perspective, but what about Jessie's side of the story?

How did Danny and Jessie get together as a couple?

What really happened between Jessie and Billy?

Who was Jessie's husband that she wound up leaving?

Find out in this free digital extra, *Mason's Dads*.

Download your free copy of **Mason's Dads** today at *BrianDavidFloyd.com/MasonsDads*.

Acknowledgements

Writing is a solitary and sometimes lonely task, but every story told is also a type of collaboration in its own unique way. It would be a great oversight on my part to not give credit to those who played a role behind the scenes in bringing *Last Wishes* to life and helping me tell the best story possible as I put the words to the page.

Almighty God – At its core, *Last Wishes* is a story about forgiveness, healing, and grace, which reflect the character and love of the Creator. I wouldn't be here without Him nor would I have the gifts and talents for storytelling if He hadn't put them in me in the first place.

Gerri Galiffa – You weren't only my neighbor for years, you were one of the best friends I've ever had. You prodded me to write this story and provided early feedback on it. Unfortunately, you left this mortal life before this book's publication. I love and miss you deeply. *(And yes one of my friends did fall in her septic tank while TPing her house)*

Phil Ham – Thank you for your time and expertise as a

nurse at Loma Linda. Nearly everything I included about the care provided to Billy in this book came directly from the information you provided me. Hopefully I got it right.

Cloyd Havens – The one friend from college who I continuously stay in touch with. Thanks for providing your legal insight into wills, trusts, and medical directives. I owe you a breakfast at Flappy Jacks.

Randy Hess – Steel guitar player extraordinaire. Thank you for giving me your time and your insight about guitars and the Nashville scene. I'm honored to be your "manager."

Phil Kellard, Stephanie Vanderham, Jennifer Beichner, Robert Slawsby, Dusty Garza, Sam Robson & Brandon Plantz – You each provided feedback and encouragement that made *Last Wishes* better. Thank you all for your friendship and your honest critique of this story as it was coming together.

Norco – The small town I grew up in that shaped me in a lot of ways. I've long wanted to tell a story set there, and while *Last Wishes* doesn't explore this unique place as much as I may have liked, Norco remains a major character and influence in this book.

Brian David Floyd
January 2020

About the Author

Brian David Floyd is the author of the rock and roll fantasy *Cloning Elvis*, the nostalgic coming-of-age *The Class of '87* (written with Robert Slawsby), the comically touching memoir *Dad Was Right*, and *The Short Stack* – a collection of his short stories.

When he's not reading or writing, Brian enjoys country dancing, exploring the United States and its history, impersonating Elvis Presley, attending epic Guns N' Roses concerts, and pretty much anything *Star Wars*.

Brian is a native of Southern California. While he's grateful for the weather, he hates the traffic.

You can learn more about Brian, what he's up to, and discover free original stories on his website: BrianDavidFloyd.com

You can also find Brian on Facebook: Brian David Floyd

Twitter: @BrianDFloyd

Instagram: BrianDFloyd

And Goodreads: Brian David Floyd

Also by Brian David Floyd

The Class of '87 (with Robert Slawsby)

Cloning Elvis

Dad Was Right: 10 Life Lessons a Father Taught His Son

The Short Stack: Four Short Stories and One Random Poem

Learn more about Brian and get free stories at
BrianDavidFloyd.com